Blotto, Twinks and the Suspicious Guests

Simon Brett

CONSTABLE

CONSTABLE

First published in hardback in Great Britain by Constable in 2022

This paperback edition published in 2022 by Constable

A CIP catalogue record for this book is available
from the British Library.

ISBN: 978-1-47213-394-6

Typeset in Palatino by Photoprint, Torquay
Printed and bound in Great Britain by Clays Ltd, Elcograf S.p.A.

Papers used by Constable are from well-managed forests and
other responsible sources.

Constable
An imprint of
Little, Brown Book Group
Carmelite House
50 Victoria Embankment
London EC4Y 0DZ

An Hachette UK Company
www.hachette.co.uk

www.littlebrown.co.uk

To Cathy,
with love

Two Old Boilers

'What, you mean the Earl does it for money?' asked Blotto, appalled. 'That's way beyond the barbed wire! What a stencher!'

It was rare for Devereux Lyminster, younger son of the late Duke of Tawcester, to express criticism of a fellow aristocrat. Centuries of the feudal system and public school (which were more or less the same thing) had inculcated in him the honourable principle of sticking together with your own kind (and treating everyone else like dirt). But then it was rare for Blotto to have heard the kind of revelation he just had about the activities of the Earl of Woking.

The person who had unleashed this bombshell on him was his sister, Lady Honoria Lyminster, known to everyone who didn't call her 'milady' as 'Twinks'. Both siblings were extraordinarily good-looking. If a Greek god were blond (and it's always hard to tell hair colour from the statues they have left to posterity), then he'd be the ideal lookalike for Blotto. The young man was in his twenties and had the figure of an athlete, honed by years of cricket and riding to hounds, at both of which sports he excelled. His tanned face boasted honest blue eyes under a thatch of wheat-coloured hair. Each feature was perfectly formed, the patrician nose, the resolute chin, and even the ears (although there was nothing between them).

But any intellectual inadequacy was more than made up for by the intelligence of his sister. Twinks was exquisitely petite, which might suggest that her brain weighed in at less than the national average, but there was no mistaking its power. Rarely, save in the Senior Common Room of St Raphael's College Oxford, did she find brains that could engage with hers on equal terms. And it was a constant source of amazement that someone so gifted intellectually could be a creature of such beauty. Also blonde, her hair was of a finer silver filigree than her brother's. Her skin had the glow of alabaster warmed by the first pink light of dawn. Her azure eyes were bottomless pools of seduction. Amorous swains fell for her with the frequency of apples thudding to the ground at the end of summer.

That evening the siblings were sitting over cocoa in Twinks's boudoir. She was not only smoking a cigarette but had also made the cocoa herself. Blotto sometimes had his breath taken away by how modern a girl his sister was. He always felt secure, though, in her boudoir, a confection of white silk and lace.

Twinks had summoned the confab to discuss the latest crisis in the Tawcester Towers' finances. It was the same old problem – the plumbing. During the early years of the twentieth century, shortcomings in that area were tolerated by guests at stately homes (unless they were Americans – and nobody with any breeding cared what Americans thought). Someone staying for a weekend house party would not be surprised by a heating system which clanked through the night like a medieval ghost army, by the fact that there was only one bathroom per twenty bedrooms, and that all the taps yielded was a thin trickle of lukewarm brown water. But though they set the bar low, weekend guests did have an expectation that, at however modest a level, the plumbing should work. And in Tawcester Towers that very rarely happened.

2

To the family resources this represented a major drain – one which, unlike most of the drains in the Lyminster ancestral home, was not blocked. Outgoings on the Tawcester Towers plumbing were at least as great as other notorious ways of losing money – like keeping a string of racehorses in training – and much less fun.

Now the main boiler, a massive, daunting contraption in one of the Tawcester Towers cellars, which looked and behaved like a terrifying, coal-gobbling monster from a medieval vision of Hell, had finally given up and exploded.

It was to devise a way of raising the cash for this emergency that Twinks had summoned Blotto to her boudoir. Humbly, he knew his role in such discussions. He would listen while his sister outlined the potential solutions and then agree vigorously when she told him which was the best one.

She gave short shrift to the idea of either her or Blotto marrying somebody enormously rich. Such a plan had frequently been suggested by their mother, the Dowager Duchess of Tawcester, but it had never come off. This was because neither of the siblings was very keen on the idea of marriage. At an early age, Twinks had made a private oath to give herself to someone she not only loved, but who also was her intellectual equal. And the chances of those two qualities coinciding in a single man, of comparable breeding to her own, were so remote that she was quite reconciled to the idea of adventurous and active spinsterhood.

As for Blotto, he feared that the permanent presence of a woman in his life might have an adverse effect on the uncomplicated love he felt for his cricket bat, his Lagonda and his hunter Mephistopheles.

The solution of raising money by criminal activity was also quickly dismissed. Although the family fortune had been built up over the centuries by various forms of licensed larceny, Blotto and Twinks both had extremely

3

high standards of morality. They believed it was wrong to steal money from anyone (except, of course, serfs, servants and tradesmen).

After once again rejecting marriage and crime to solve their problems, Twinks had moved on to the financial activities of the Earl of Woking, which had prompted such revulsion from Blotto. The peer in question was owner of Clusters, the nearest stately home to Tawcester Towers, less than fifty miles away and in the same county of Tawcestershire.

Between the two families there had always existed a rivalry. Had the earldom existed during the Wars of the Roses, this would have found expression with battleaxes and broadswords, but the Woking line wasn't around then. The title had only been created in the sixteenth century, so the Lyminsters had never questioned their superiority over such *parvenus*.

The rivalry now took the gentle form of cricket matches and poaching domestic staff – particularly chefs – from each other.

'So, tell me again, Twinks me old soup-strainer, what has that lump of toadspawn Woking been up to?'

'He's been renting out parts of Clusters for private functions!'

'What, you mean actually *charging money* to his guests?'

'Bong on the nose, Blotters! He's been charging money for people he invites to shooting parties, weekends . . . even cricket matches.'

The news of this final perfidy prompted a rare display of foul language (in front of a lady) from her brother. 'Broken biscuits!' he said. 'The four-faced filcher! Imagine charging money for your old muffin-toasters from Eton to come and play cricket!'

'The Earl of Woking didn't actually go to Eton,' Twinks mentioned cautiously. She was a little anxious about her brother's likely reaction.

'Didn't he, by Denzil?'

'No, he was at Winchester.'

'Poor greengage,' murmured Blotto, expressing his natural sympathy for the afflicted.

'Anyway, what Woking's doing is worse than that, Blotto me old wisp of navel lint. He's not charging his muffin-toasters. The people he's getting to pay aren't our sort of people.'

'Not our sort of people!' came the thunderstruck echo.

'No.'

'Toad-in-the-hole! You mean they haven't got titles?'

'No.'

'They didn't go to private schools?'

'No.'

'You're saying that the Earl of Woking has been inviting oikish sponge-worms into his ancestral home, giving them hospitality as if they were the genuine article – and making them pay for the privilege?'

'Give that pony a rosette!' said Twinks.

'Something must be done about this!' said Blotto grimly.

The traditional method by which domestic harmony was maintained in aristocratic circles was ensuring that family members saw as little of each other as possible. This had always, since the founding of the feudal system, been particularly true of husbands and wives. Though a little inevitable commingling occurred for the purposes of procreation, recreational sex was generally outsourced. And conversational intercourse was restricted to occasions when protocol demanded that the couple should be seen together, in other words when other people were present. The idea that an aristocratic couple should engage in voluntary dialogue when on their own was bizarre and unthinkable.

The closeness between Blotto and Twinks was therefore unusual in people of their breeding. And communication between the two of them and their elder brother, the current Duke of Tawcester, was as rare as a chin at a Hunt Ball.

(On the matter of chins, it should be noted that, unfortunately for Loofah, as the Duke was universally known, his younger brother had monopolised the family allocation. Whereas the outline of Blotto's jaw mirrored the Greeks' sculptures of their gods, there was an undeviating straight line between Loofah's lower lip and his collar stud.)

Also present in the Blue Morning Room that morning was the current Duchess. Loofah's wife, known universally as Sloggo, had the translucent pallor of an uncooked shrimp. Indeed, there seemed to be an unacknowledged competition between husband and wife as to which of them could look the more anaemic. Had there been such a contest in the racing calendar as the Anaemia Stakes, they would have dead-heated on the line.

Sloggo's pallor may have been in part due to the strains of childbearing. As the wife of a Duke, she had recognised early into her marriage that her aim in life was the production of a male heir. So far, her ambitions in that direction had not been fulfilled, though the Duke and Duchess's quarters in Tawcester Towers were littered with innumerable daughters. The couple's sense of duty, however, did not allow them to give up the quest, and their continuing vigorous and joyless attempts to manufacture the missing male heir perhaps accounted for their mutual pastiness.

The fact that the entire generation of the Lyminster family had been summoned to the Blue Morning Room was a measure of the occasion's importance. And a demonstration, if one were needed, of the powerful will of the three aristocratic siblings' mother, the Dowager Duchess of Tawcester.

In descriptions of this monument to the effects of inbreeding, 'battleaxe', 'trout' and 'old boiler' have been used, but the word that it is hardest to avoid is 'dinosaur'. At the risk of being discourteous to fossils, not only did the

Dowager Duchess share certain features with exhibits in the Natural History Museum, it was also easy to believe that she had been in existence since the Triassic Period. Her habitual expression made the North Face of the Eiger look hospitable. The maternal instinct was a weakness that had, over generations, been bred out of her. Her attitude to her children was that, since each had been born with a silver spoon in his or her mouth, she was not required to add any further indulgences, like affection, to their cutlery drawers.

Even Twinks found her mother daunting, and the two male offspring were frankly terrified of her. Sloggo was equally cowed, so it was no surprise that nobody in the Blue Morning Room spoke until the Dowager Duchess herself had initiated the conversation.

'It will not have escaped your attention,' she began, 'not even your attention, Loofah and Blotto, which most things manage to escape . . .' (She had no illusions about her sons' intellectual abilities.) '. . . that Tawcester Towers is currently boilerless. And while it has always been my belief that getting cold never did anybody any harm, and that excessive bathing tends to weaken the protective layers of the skin . . .' (Here she was simply affirming two articles of faith with which ladies of her breeding had grown up.) '. . . the lack of hot water for the kitchen staff to use in cleaning the crockery and cutlery could possibly be injurious to the family's health.

'This is a particular danger at this time of year. Though still clement enough now in early September, the English weather does not allow me to relish the prospect of a winter without hot water.

'It is for this reason that I have summoned you all here this morning.'

'You mean, Mater,' said Twinks, considerably quicker on the uptake than other representatives of her generation present, 'that you want us to come up with some spoffing tasty wheezette as to how we can get the old jingle-jangle to mend the boiler?'

This was familiar territory. The usual reason for a summons to the Blue Morning Room was to offer solutions to the perennial problem of the Tawcester Towers plumbing. And, indeed, many of Blotto and Twinks's exotic and life-threatening adventures had begun with just such a briefing.

Twinks was therefore surprised at her mother's reply. 'No,' boomed the Dowager Duchess. 'I have brought you all here to show you how things should be done, how things used to be done before this benighted country succumbed to the infection of Socialism. There is someone I wish to introduce you to, someone who will immediately solve our current problem.'

'Oh?' asked Loofah timorously. 'You mean a money-lender?' then, even more fearful, 'Is it a banker?'

That would have made sense. Reliance on bankers and money-lenders to sort out mortgages, overdrafts and other such tedious details had a long tradition in the British aristocracy.

'No,' pronounced the Dowager Duchess, pulling the bell-rope conveniently placed near her throne as she spoke, 'it is not a banker. It is a plumber.'

An audible shudder ran through the family assembly. The last word was not one that had been heard before in the Blue Morning Room.

2

The Right Sort of Workman

The man whom the Tawcester Towers butler Grimshaw, summoned by the Dowager Duchess's bell, ushered into her presence, did not look as though he had ever been in a space like the Blue Morning Room before. He wore a white overall and white gloves. He was literally 'cap in hand', in his case a flat one in indeterminate brown tweed. The black boots which sank into the pile of the carpet had been cleaned specially for the occasion. Beneath his nose was a small unnecessary moustache and his hair was slicked back with some plebeian equivalent of pomade. Premature baldness had deprived him of a forelock, but if he'd had one, he would undoubtedly have tugged it.

Yet, though he showed appropriate deference, the man did not appear overawed by his surroundings. Clearly, he had met and gained the respect of the Dowager Duchess before, and knew that, unlike her family, he had no reason to fear the most fearsome presence in the room.

Having granted Grimshaw leave to withdraw, she announced, 'This, children, is Mr Rodney Perkins. He is a plumber.'

They did not know whether to be more astonished by her calling them 'children', or by the continuing shock at the fact that the Dowager Duchess actually knew a plumber. No doubt, amongst the circle of aristocratic crones and cronies whom she so constantly disparaged, recommendations might be exchanged for jewellers, couturiers, or milliners, but not for plumbers. Booking such menials was surely the province of some minor functionary like the butler or the estate manager?

And yet here was the Dowager Duchess of Tawcester introducing a plumber, whom she had clearly met before, into the Blue Morning Room of Tawcester Towers! Whatever next, they all wondered. At some time in the future, might the heir to the British throne go off with an America divorcée? The idea was no less incongruous.

'Mr Perkins,' the Dowager Duchess continued, 'has been generous enough to inspect the boiler in the Tawcester Towers cellar and pronounced it to be ... what was the word you used, Mr Perkins?'

'Defunct, Your Grace.'

'"Defunct", children, is a word which suggests the impossibility of revival. Rather as the word "extinct" might be used to describe a peerage which has run out of heirs. So, the boiler in our cellar cannot be repaired. Is that correct, Mr Perkins?'

'It is indeed, Your Grace. The only means by which hot water can be reintroduced to the building is by the installation of a new boiler.'

'And that is a task, Mr Perkins, that you are capable of performing?'

'Undoubtedly. I have installed many boilers, Your Grace, in many properties, though few have been as extensive as Tawcester Towers.'

'But the scale of the task does not deter you?'

'Your Grace, it would be an honour for a humble artisan like myself to work on a building whose history is so intertwined with that of our noble nation.'

Great galumphing goatherds, Twinks asked herself, what has he been reading? Or what has he been taking? She didn't believe that plumbers usually spoke like that.

'And how long do you imagine such work would take to complete, Mr Perkins?'

'Given the extensive network of radiators in the building – not to mention two bathrooms . . .' (This, up until the close of the previous century, had been reckoned an adequate – not to say generous – allocation for a structure the size of Tawcester Towers.) '. . . I would estimate that the job could be finished within four weeks.'

'And when would you be able to commence your travails, Mr Perkins?'

'Next Monday, Your Grace,' he replied, with a promptitude which Twinks was perceptive enough to realise (though her brothers and Sloggo weren't) implied a degree of prior agreement, if not actual rehearsal, between her mother and the plumber.

'And while you were working on our boiler, Mr Perkins,' asked the Dowager Duchess, 'neither you nor your fellow artisans would go off to work on tasks for other employers?'

'Certainly not, Your Grace.' No one else in the room had sufficient knowledge of dealing with the artisan class to recognise how unlikely a promise this was. In the credo of any workman, going off to work on projects for other people was an article of faith.

'Then, Mr Perkins,' said the Dowager Duchess magnanimously, 'we would appear to have concluded our business.'

'Very good, Your Grace.'

But before the plumber could make his departure, there was a sound of diffident clearing from the unchinned throat of the Duke of Tawcester. It was so unlike Loofah to draw attention to himself, that Blotto and Twinks listened with interest to what he had to say.

'Erm . . . don't want to poke me cue in the wrong pocket,' the Duke began hesitantly, 'but it brushes the old braincells that there's an "i" that hasn't been dotted here.'

'And what would that be?' his mother demanded imperiously.

'Well, Mater,' Loofah continued tentatively, 'fact is, there's something that hasn't been given a mench ... though it's not something boddoes should clunter on about in mixed company.'

'Loofah,' boomed the Dowager Duchess, 'the occasions are exceedingly rare on which I glean any reward for all the effort I put into ensuring that you had a proper upbringing ...' A bit rich, coming from someone who had delegated all such functions to nursemaids, governesses and the English public school system. 'But this moment is one of them.'

So unused was the Duke of Tawcester to praise from his mother that he could only gape hopelessly. Had he had a jaw, it would have dropped.

'You know, Loofah, what is conversationally appropriate when ladies are present. And I will leave you to sort out the relevant arrangements with Mr Perkins. Twinks, Sloggo, we will leave the room.'

And, like a galleon in full sail, with daughter and daughter-in-law in her wake, the Dowager Duchess did just that.

The three women seemed to have sucked all the Blue Morning Room's oxygen out with them and it took the three men a moment to get their breath back. Even then, quite a long silence ensued.

The fact was that neither Blotto nor Loofah had much experience of talking about the old jingle-jangle, certainly not with someone so different in breeding as a plumber. Their upbringing had taught them little about money, but generations spent taking advantage of the less fortunate, both at home and abroad, had built in them the assumption that there'd always be some of the stuff around.

When informed by tedious people like accountants that there wasn't any left, their first reaction remained to borrow some. When that ran out, borrow some more. It seemed to work. Generally speaking, over the centuries Lyminsters had managed by this method to fund such harmless pastimes as cricket and hunting, not to mention losing vast sums at the gaming tables and on the horses. It was all in accordance with the fine traditions of the British aristocracy.

The only problem arose when the lowlife who'd lent the money were ungracious enough to ask for it back. This, in the view of Blotto, Loofah and their like, was not cricket. Way beyond the barbed wire, in fact. Didn't the stenchers have any sense of honour, any respect for their betters?

So, negotiating with a plumber was a situation for which neither Lyminster brother had any training.

Loofah started the ball rolling. 'Erm . . .' he began. This was his opening gambit in almost any situation. 'What the Mater was cluntering on about, Mr Perkins, was the matter of . . . erm . . . not to shimmy around the shrubbery, the matter of . . . well . . . erm . . . Without fiddling round the fir trees, the subject in question is . . . erm . . . You tell him, Blotto.'

'Broken biscuits,' mumbled the younger brother, thrown by this development.

'Go on, Blotters,' Loofah urged him, 'uncage the ferrets.'

'Erm . . .' Blotto began safely, echoing his brother. 'Mr Perkins, the fact is . . . that what we need to gab about . . . to take the thing down to its frilly drawers . . . is . . . erm . . . not to put too fine a point on it . . . is . . . erm . . .'

'Money?' Rodney Perkins suggested, only trying to be helpful.

The aristocratic brothers exchanged looks of equal shock and flabbergastation. Though the word must have been heard before in the Blue Morning Room, it had never been uttered there by someone with the lowly status of a plumber.

Blotto gulped and agreed, 'Yes, Mr Perkins. I am talking about the old jingle-jangle, the golden gravy, if you prefer. Presumably, you're one of those grasping greengages who expects someone to be footing the finance for your faddling?'

'Yes, milord,' he agreed. 'I do expect to be paid for my work.'

Blotto's noble brow wrinkled. 'I was rather afraid that might be the partridge you were popping.' He sighed. It wasn't the moment to bemoan the decline of the feudal system. Things had been so much simpler then. The aristocracy had survived by exploiting everyone else and no one had thought to question the justice of the arrangement. Not all changes wrought by time, Blotto thought with another sigh, had been beneficial.

Getting no further response, Rodney Perkins went on, 'Mind you, I am aware of the honour of working on an edifice as noble and historic as Tawcester Towers.'

Edifice? Twinks, had she still been present, would have raised an eyebrow at his choice of word. Did the average par-for-the-course plumber talk about edifices?

'Good ticket,' said Blotto, approving the plumber's sentiments. 'Give that pony a rosette.'

'And,' Rodney Perkins continued humbly, 'I am also aware of the honour of working for a family as distinguished as the Lyminsters.'

'Give that pony another rosette! A great big red one!' said Blotto. 'Eh, Loofah?'

'And a Best Turned-Out Award!' his brother enthused.

Another silence. Since Loofah was clearly not going to take any more initiative now than he had in any other area of his life (except, of course, in the business of regularly impregnating Sloggo with another girl), Blotto continued the interrogation. 'And, Mr Perkins, do you feel that an honour equal to be being employed by the Lyminsters is to be working on one of the finest ancestral homes in the history of our great nation?'

'That goes without saying, milord. Since the possibility of my securing this commission was first proposed, I have awoken every morning glowing with the thought of it. A state of mind to which, should you require corroboration, Mrs Perkins could readily attest.'

Had Twinks still been present, she would once again have asked herself about the plumber's reading matter. His speech was surprisingly orotund for one of his station. She would also have pounced on his reference to when 'securing this commission was first proposed'. How had the Dowager Duchess made initial contact with this supremely eloquent plumber?

But Blotto was not as quick as his sister at realising the ramifications of events, so he went on simply, 'Mr Perkins, would the honour of working for the Lyminsters make you turn a Nelson's eye to any delay in our coming up with the old jingle-jangle?'

'I would not, of course, milord, think it appropriate for someone of my humble station in life to draw attention to any such oversight.'

'Good ticket!' said Blotto enthusiastically, as he pressed on, 'And you wouldn't ever think the Lyminsters were selling you up the river for a handful of winkle shells . . . ?

'Such a thought would never have the temerity to cross my mind,' the plumber responded piously.

'. . . if the next step in the staircase turned out to be your bill never being paid?'

'Milord,' Rodney Perkins replied, 'though such an outcome might cause me temporary embarrassment, I would still be honoured to have played my part in the procedures by which the English aristocracy have traditionally conducted their business.'

'He's a Grade A foundation stone!' Blotto announced to Twinks later that day. They were once again drinking cocoa in her boudoir and he was bringing her up to date with events in the Blue Morning Room after the ladies had retired. 'To hear an oikish sponge-worm like Mr Perkins say the things he was saying restores a boddo's faith in humanity.'

'You really told him the tale? You raised the poss of him replacing the boiler and then getting none of the golden gravy?'

'I certainly did, by Denzil!'

'Was Loofah any help?'

Twinks didn't really know why she'd raised the question, and was unsurprised when Blotto said, 'No.' It was a close-run thing, but she sometimes thought the older Lyminster brother had even less between his ears than the younger.

'No, it really is the lark's larynx,' Blotto continued enthusing. 'To come across the kind of servility that seemed to have gone out with the crinoline. Rodney Perkins is an artisan of the old school. His first thought is not of the spondulicks. He knows his place – down with the serfs, villeins, accountants, solicitors, and other dregs of humanity. He recognises the proper order of things. He's as happy as a duck in orange to be giving his services to his betters. He isn't obsessed with the old jingle-jangle. If more of the peasant classes had Rodney Perkins's attitude to their duties, then everything would be pure creamy éclair, wouldn't it, Twinks?'

Twinks pretended to agree. She couldn't bear to put a damper on her brother's naïve optimism. It would have felt as antisocial as locking the lid of a Jack-in-the-Box. But deep down, she thought anything that sounded too good to be true generally was. Rodney Perkins sounded too good to be true. Something about this particular Stilton was distinctly iffy.

She would watch future developments in the boiler saga with considerable circumspection.

A Call to Clusters

Twinks was restless and out of sorts. Her giant brain required constant nourishment and, currently, it was feeling starved. She needed a project, an adventure, something with which to engage the power of that mighty cerebellum.

Much as she loved her younger brother, she had never, from the nursery onward, looked to him for intellectual stimulus. The same went for the rest of the family and staff at Tawcester Towers. She had very quickly outstripped the academic achievements of her many governesses, being fluent by the age of five in seven languages.

Her brilliance was unsullied by the interference of any university though, had she been to one, she might have met more people whose attainments matched her own. She did keep up a regular correspondence, and occasionally met with, Professor Erasmus Holofernes of St Raphael's College Oxford, reckoned to be one of the most impressive intellects in the known world. But even he, on occasion, had to admit that Twinks was too clever for him.

She had therefore, from an early age, learnt to make her own entertainment. And, while other young girls might have built up collections of soft toys or Dolls of All the Nations, Twinks had bought books. By the time she was in her teens, the Reference Section in her boudoir far exceeded the resources of the Tawcestershire Library Service. This vast array of printed material helped to increase her knowledge even further and gave her new subjects to explore. Sometimes she would occupy her mind with the conundrums of science, sometimes with solving hitherto unsolved mathematical theorems, but her favoured means of staving off boredom was translation.

Twinks always had some such project on the go and, after Blotto had left her boudoir, she returned to the current one. She was translating *Three Men in a Boat* into the Mongolic Khalkha dialect. This was not because she believed there to be much demand for the *oeuvre* of Jerome K. Jerome in Mongolia – and indeed she would have been appalled by the suggestion of her translation's commercial exploitation. Her activity was no more than a diversion, just as her contemporaries might play solitaire, read a whodunnit or embroider a handkerchief.

Twinks was in the process of selecting the most euphonious words in Khalkha for 'Irish stew' when she heard a tap on the door of her boudoir. She granted admission to a footman who brought her an envelope on a silver salver.

It was an invitation for the following weekend to a house party at Clusters. The perfect opportunity to find out what the Earl of Woking was really up to.

Blotto, it turned out, had received the same invitation. His first instinct was to make some excuse. The Earl of Woking, he happened to know, had almost as many daughters as Loofah and Sloggo. And Blotto was wary of families with an excess of unmarried girls. He had received too many invitations whose ulterior motive was to nail him into the coffin of matrimony.

Also, he had another commitment on the relevant weekend. On the Sunday, he would be leading the Tawcester Towers cricket team in a match against the Marquis of

Hartlepool's travelling side, known as the Irrelevancies. In the most recent fixture, the Marquis's lot had had the nerve to beat the home team. Honour had to be satisfied. On behalf of Tawcester Towers, Blotto must avenge the defeat. So, he was all set to decline the summons to Clusters.

Twinks, however, would not allow him to turn down the invitation. She was skilled at seeing off avid young women – and their scheming mothers – who eyed her brother for his breeding potential. And she saw the advantage of having another pair of eyes – regardless of the quality of the brain to which they were connected – to see what was going on at Clusters.

Blotto had, however, got his way to some extent. The prospect of a whole weekend as the Earl of Woking's guest was more than either sibling could contemplate. Even without the imperative of the cricket, there had to be a particularly good reason for Blotto to spend a night anywhere other than in the damp sheets of his own bed in Tawcester Towers. And Twinks was aware that a little of the Earl of Woking and his family went a long way. So, it was agreed that they should only go to Clusters for the dinner on the Saturday evening and return home thereafter.

Blotto was all for driving the pair of them over in his Lagonda (one, as everyone knows, of the three most adored non-human objects in his life, the other two being his cricket bat and his hunter Mephistopheles). But Twinks, remembering her brother's propensity for dealing with uncongenial social situations by getting profoundly wobbulated, decreed that they should be driven to and from Clusters. To save the bother of changing, they would travel in their dinner clothes, Blotto in immaculate tails, Twinks in an enchanting creation in dove-grey silk, which showed her perfect white-stockinged legs to full advantage. From her slender wrist, as ever, would dangle her sequinned reticule.

It was arranged that, for the event in two weeks' time, they would be driven to Clusters in one of the Tawcester Towers Rolls-Royces, and that the driver would be one of the Tawcester Towers chauffeurs, Corky Froggett.

Corky Froggett had never really recovered from what he referred to as 'the recent dust-up against the Hun'. Unlike most of those involved, who couldn't wait for the hostilities to end, the chauffeur only wished they could have gone on longer. The 1918 Armistice had come as a great disappointment to him. He regarded himself as a supremely efficient killing machine and did not take kindly to having the licence to practise his craft taken away. It was a profound shock for him to discover that what he'd been so innocently getting on with for four years, on behalf of His Majesty, had suddenly become a criminal activity.

But, not being by nature one to dwell on the reverses of his life, and deprived of opportunities to lay down his life for his country, he made a slight shift of allegiance and grew increasingly keen on laying down his life for his employers, the family at Tawcester Towers. In particular, the height of his ambition had become the laying down of his life for the young master, Devereux Lyminster.

Corky had been involved in many of the aristocratic siblings' adventures, sharing their hardships and dangers, though not yet, sadly, to the point of being killed protecting them. But he lived in hope.

The chauffeur was invaluable to Blotto and Twinks, not only in his bodyguard capacity, but also as a conduit to life below stairs at Tawcester Towers. He had close relationships (in some cases *very* close relationships) with many of the domestic staff and could always be relied on to pass on the latest gossip. Since there existed a strange kind of bush telegraph between the staff of other stately homes in the vicinity, Corky Froggett was also an invaluable source of information about the Lyminsters' fellow members of the peerage. Like the Earl of Woking.

As soon as the name was raised on the drive to Clusters, the chauffeur warmed to his task. 'Well, milord and milady, I do have an insight into that particular household. A kitchen maid from the Earl of Woking's establishment has recently joined the domestic staff at Tawcester Towers and, while I was showing her the ropes, she told me quite a lot about goings-on there.'

Blotto and Twinks were both far too tactful to ask what kind of ropes a chauffeur might be showing a kitchen maid.

'According to the young lady in question,' Corky went on, 'there have been strange events occurring at Clusters.'

'What kind of strange events?' asked Twinks eagerly. 'Come on, Corkers, uncage the ferrets.'

'Events,' he replied sonorously, 'that have no rational explanation.'

'What, you mean,' asked Blotto, 'like why boddoes go to any school other than Eton?'

'No, milord,' said Corky. 'Even more mysterious than that.'

'Oh, stop jiggling my kneecap, Corky. There's nothing in the whole spoffing world more mysterious than that.'

'I refer,' Corky intoned, 'to events from . . . the Other Side.'

'You're not talking about those stenchers from Harrow, are you?'

'No, milord.'

Impatiently, Twinks cut through all this. 'You are referring, Corkers, to supernatural phenomena?'

'I am indeed, milady.'

'So, according to your little thimble of a kitchen maid, what fumacious manifestations have there been at Clusters?'

'"Fumacious" is very definitely the word, milady. The guest rooms have been the hosts to suspicious guests.

Spectral apparitions have appeared ... spectrally. Armoured knights have been heard to clank in the night-time. Statues have been dashed down from their plinths. The family silver has been hurled by invisible hands against the panelled walls of the Great Hall. The family portraits have come to life and uttered curses against the Earl of Woking and all his kin. Headless figures have promenaded in the Long Gallery. In a word, milady, Clusters is haunted!'

Twinks looked more animated than she had for some weeks, as she murmured on a long breath the word, 'Larksissimo!'

Clusters could not boast the antiquity of Tawcester Towers. It was a perfect Elizabethan edifice, with long windows and – appropriately – clusters of tall, barley-sugar chimneys. Since the house was not yet four hundred years old, however, the Lyminsters regarded it as somewhat *nouveau riche*.

The same went for the family that occupied the premises. The earldom of Woking had been created by Henry VIII, as an expression of gratitude for the family's help in funding various divorces. But the first Earl did not come from aristocratic lineage. His ancestors had no distinguished history of mutilating serfs from the Norman Conquest onwards. In fact, he had made the money he so lavishly spread around from ... the rest of the peerage had difficulty in saying the word ... *trade*. He had been an importer of silk. And, though he and his descendants, with a view to blending imperceptibly into the aristocracy, very quickly stopped actually working, the taint remained. To a family like the Lyminsters, the Earls of Woking would never be more than jumped-up tradesmen.

And now to that stigma had been added the allegation that the current Earl was reverting to type by opening Clusters up to commercial exploitation. Blotto and Twinks could not wait to find evidence of this latest breach of the *noblesse oblige* principle.

Corky Froggett brought the Rolls-Royce to a graceful halt in the gravel directly in front of the main doors. After decanting his aristocratic load, he drove round to the garages. Then he made his way to the servant's entrance to see if he could pick up where he had left off on a previous visit with yet another kitchen maid.

Blotto and Twinks, having had their coats taken from them, were ushered to where pre-prandial drinks were being served, which was of course the Main Library. Twinks entered with some excitement. As everyone of her breeding knew, at country house weekend parties, the Library was where the murders took place.

Because most of the guests had already been at Clusters for more than twenty-four hours, there was no elaborate greeting ceremony for the new arrivals. So Blotto and Twinks were able to slip into the Main Library almost unobserved, lift glasses of champagne from outheld trays and take in the social scene.

The first striking thing was how many guests there were. The second was the kind of guests they were. Blotto was not observant about that kind of thing, but Twinks's finely tuned nose was more sensitive. And the one thing it couldn't smell in that assembly was breeding.

The Earl of Woking, a rubber ball of a man, whose white waistcoat strained to contain his prominent stomach, swept towards them. 'Devereux, Honoria, welcome to Clusters!' He gestured to a tall, saturnine figure beside him. 'Allow me to introduce my Master of the Revels!'

23

4

Master of the Revels

'The Master of the Revels,' said the tall man smoothly, 'was the person appointed to arrange courtly entertainments. The post dates from the fourteenth century.'

'We know that,' came the haughty response from Twinks. 'There were Lyminsters around back then.'

This was not only a put-down to the Master of the Revels, it was also a reminder to the Earl of Woking that his peerage dated only from the sixteenth century, and that the Lyminsters – unlike some people – were not just jumped-up silk peddlers. They had got their titles the respectable, traditional way – by killing people in battle and bankrolling the king with money extorted from the lower classes.

The stuffy way in which the Earl completed the introductions showed that he was aware of the slight. His Master of the Revels, it turned out, was called Mr Diamond. It was to be assumed that he had a first name but, given his menial position, it was not mentioned.

'Mr Diamond,' the Earl went on, 'is having a great impact on the social entertainments offered here at Clusters. Maybe you should consider making a similar appointment at Tawcester Towers?'

'That is an idea,' said Twinks with icy *hauteur*, 'that

should, at the earliest opportunity, be allowed to shrivel on the twig.'

At that moment, they were joined by a man as tall as the Master of the Revels. Dark and saturnine, he comported himself with that languor which might denote a genuine aristocrat. The Earl introduced him to Blotto and Twinks as Baron Chipping Norton. They had never heard of him, but then they didn't claim to know every other member of the British aristocracy. And, given the pace at which Prime Minister Lloyd George had recently been selling off peerages, it was hard to keep up with every new addition.

'Hello,' the Baron drawled, turning on Twinks one of the two looks from men she had, over the years, come to recognise instantly. The first was goggle-eyed gaping, particularly from chinless young aristocrats, which indicated that the sufferer had immediately fallen for her like a midshipman from a crow's nest. She had seen that look from every unmarried man in the English peerage who had had the good fortune to meet her (and a good few of the married ones too). Twinks was rare among dukes' daughters in having looks which belonged more to the boudoir than the stable. Her charms offered the prospect for ardent young men of finding their sex lives and their married lives in one person (something unusual in the aristocracy).

The second look she had become accustomed to was one of cool, controlled, but undiluted, lust. That was the more dangerous, and it was the one that Baron Chipping Norton had focused on her. Men who gave her that look tended to be tenacious and devious. Also, annoyingly, they were the kind of men Twinks was attracted to. She always managed to thwart their ambitions eventually, but the process was longer and more difficult than simply swatting down the standard-issue amorous swain.

It was clear from the slight sneer on Baron Chipping Norton's face that he knew what she was thinking. The battle lines had been drawn.

25

But hostilities were not going to be opened immediately. With a curt nod to Blotto and Twinks, the Baron drew the Master of the Revels to one side and engaged in a heated but, unfortunately, inaudible discussion with him. From their postures, it appeared that Mr Diamond was being berated for some shortcoming. The Earl of Woking looked a little put out, as if he would have liked to be included in their conversation.

Unable to do that, he continued to praise his Master of the Revels. 'Mr Diamond has organised a busy programme of events for our guests today.'

'Surely,' said Twinks, 'you're using the wrong spoffing word. A "guest" is someone a "host" has invited to share his hospitality. It is not someone who's been invited to pay for the privilege of sharing the host's hospitality.'

The Earl of Woking was clearly seething, but he managed to stay polite as he said, 'I just think we are extremely fortunate to live in the circumstances we do. And it is only right that those born less fortunate should be allowed an insight into our way of life.'

'See "How The Other Half Live" . . . ?' suggested Twinks.

'Exactly. And thus, perhaps do something to level out the differences between the classes.'

'Toad-in-the-hole!' said Blotto, appalled by the idea. '"What's the point of having privilege if everyone else has it too? That sounds like spoffing Socialism!'

'Not if they're stumping up the jingle-jangle for it,' said Twinks. 'If they were being given the entertainment for free, that might be Socialism. This is just old-fashioned money-grubbing.' She turned a charming smile on their host. 'So, what was involved in Mr Diamond's "programme of events" for today?'

'He organised a guided tour of the Long Gallery,' the Earl of Woking replied, 'so that our guests, none of whom have any history . . .'

'Like the Americans . . . ?' suggested Blotto.

'Exactly. So, seeing our family portraits in the Long Gallery would give them an inkling of what having some history feels like.'

'Spoffing generous,' said Twinks drily.

'And then the butler took them on a tour we called "Both Sides of the Green Baize Door".'

'Why in the name of snitchrags did he do that?' asked Twinks. 'To make them realise their place in the pecking order?'

'Which is "Below Stairs",' Blotto asserted fervently.

The Earl of Woking did not appear to be enjoying the conversation. He shifted the subject slightly to heap more praise on his Master of the Revels. 'It was also Mr Diamond's suggestion that we should have a jazz band playing during our pre-prandial drinks.'

Such had been the hubbub when they arrived that neither Blotto nor Twinks had been aware of the syncopated rhythms emerging from the corner of the Main Library (the corner, in fact, which used to house a desk, ideal for the sprawling-across of a murder victim, with a jewelled dagger protruding from his or her back). But now they did listen, Twinks observed that the jazz band was rather good. Blotto, whose ears were of the finest Cornish tin, was not qualified to have an opinion on the matter.

'Don't you think,' asked the Earl enthusiastically, 'that a band like this is the kind of thing to make a dinner party more fun?'

Here was a matter on which Blotto did have an opinion, based on long, tedious experiences at Tawcester Towers. 'But dinner parties,' he commented, 'aren't mean to be spoffing *fun*. They are to be endured, not enjoyed.'

The *placement* had seated Twinks next to an unmarried man, who might have been attractive to the kind of woman who liked her beefcake chunky. But Twinks, forever in search of intellectual empathy, found none. He didn't even

27

bore her with the subjects she was used to being bored with on such occasions, cricket and hunting. His breeding was so minimal that he actually bored her by talking about money, about buying shares at cat's meat prices in times of financial turmoil and sitting back to watch their value increase in times of plenty. Such subject matter at the dinner table was so far beyond the barbed wire that Twinks felt no compunction about ignoring him completely.

The young man in question, needless to say, had instantly fallen for her like a guardsman in a heatwave. Twinks was so used to such responses that she hardly noticed them any more. It was a minor irritation on the level of a mosquito bite.

On her other side, however, there was someone who promised to be more interesting. At the dinner table, some member of the Clusters domestic staff – most probably the Master of the Revels – had introduced a novelty. On the handle of the largest knife at each place setting, in what should have been ivory but was clearly some inferior material, had been etched the name of the individual seated there. The letters were inlaid with what should have been silver but was also some inferior material.

Twinks was appalled by this innovation. The knives had clearly been purpose-made, and to her the idea of using cutlery one hadn't inherited was appallingly crass. It was also a positive invitation to the guests to take the knives with them as souvenirs. Twinks found it offensive to all standards of decorum, and totally different from the aristocratic pilfering of family silver which took place at all country house weekend parties.

The uncultivated innovation did, however, have one thing going for it, enabling each guest to identify their neighbours at table far more easily than by peering at the traditional *placement* card.

His knife revealed that the name of the man sitting on Twinks's right was 'Sir Percy Sparkes, Bart.'. Obviously, a Baronet was not a proper member of the aristocracy, but his conversation promised to have more substance than that of the money bore on her other side. First, though, Twinks had to find out a little about his family.

'Are you one of the Shropshire Sparkeses,' she asked, 'who've been Masters of Foxhounds of the Grotleigh Hunt for the past three centuries?'

'No,' the Baronet replied. 'I am one of the Surrey Sparkeses, who've run a linoleum factory in Staines for the past twenty years.'

'And what,' asked Twinks haughtily, 'is linoleum?' It was one of the few words in the English language that she had never heard before.

'It's a floor covering.'

'A floor covering?' Twinks echoed disdainfully. 'You mean you are a carpet seller?'

'Not exactly,' said Sir Percy Sparkes. 'Can you imagine a carpet made from solidified linseed oil?'

'Not in seven centuries,' said Twinks, appalled by the very idea.

'Well, I can assure you, Lady Honoria, that it's very efficient and hard-wearing. Not to say decorative.'

'I find that hard to believe.'

'Oh, you should believe it, Lady Honoria. What's more, it's made me lots of . . .' Rather than speak the word, Sir Percy rubbed his thumb speedily across his forefingers.

Twinks, though she knew more or less everything, was far too well brought-up ever to have seen the international mime for money, so she hazarded a guess at his meaning. 'Breadcrumbs? Are you telling me that this fumacious linoleum has made you lots of breadcrumbs?'

'No, no, no. Where've you spent your life?'

'Clearly nowhere where I might have met anyone like you.'

'Your loss, Lady Honoria. What linoleum has made me is not breadcrumbs. It is money . . . mazuma, spondulicks, the old jingle-jangle.'

How horracious, thought Twinks. This one is just as bad as the lump of toadspawn to the other side. She determined that, for the rest of the dinner, she would speak to neither of them.

But Sir Percy Sparkes seemed happy to continue talking, without requiring any response from his listener. 'It's money that's brought me everything I need in life. How do you think I got the baronetcy? A few bob in the right pockets. Prime Minister Lloyd George always happy to oblige, if the price is right. Soon I'm going to trade up to an earldom. I've bought a stately home, too, which covers most of Wiltshire. And a Scottish castle, thousands of acres, deer forests, grouse moors, salmon fishing, the lot. You can get anything if you've got enough of the old mazuma.'

The Baronet suddenly looked at the young woman beside him. 'I could get you for the right price.'

'I can assure you,' said Twinks, her voice uncannily like her mother's, 'that you couldn't "get" me if you had in your possession all the gold reserves of the Bank of England!'

'Only a matter of time,' said Sir Percy Sparkes, with a complacent grin.

Twinks shuddered.

5

A Man with a Secret

The *placement* seemed to have given Blotto a more interesting dinner companion. To his right sat one of the Earl's stable of unmarried daughters, whose coquettish attempts to charm he studiously ignored. But on his left was a young man with a haunted look and something troubling him which he seemed eager to get off his chest. 'Have you got a title?' he hissed at Blotto.

'Well, the old Pater was a Duke of Tawcester.'

'So, are you the Duke now?'

'No, that's older bro. Current Duke. We call him Loofah.'

'For any reason?'

'Reason?' Blotto looked puzzled.

'Yes, I mean, does he look like a loofah?'

'No,' said Blotto, thinking this was a strange line of questioning. In families like the Lyminsters, nicknames didn't have a reason, they were just given to people randomly.

'Well, I'm glad you're the genuine article.' The young man looked shiftily around him. 'Because a lot of the people here aren't.'

'Are you saying they're not people?'

'No. They're not the *right sort* of real people.'

'Ah.' Blotto understood that. 'Some oikish sponge-worms seem to have crept in under the golden curtain?'

'You can say that again.'

'All right, if you insist. "Some oikish sponge-worms seem to have—"'

'No, no. I didn't mean that. Listen.' The young man brought his head closer to Blotto's and whispered, 'I'm Dicky.'

'Oh, I'm sorry to hear that,' said Blotto. 'What's wrong with you? Heart?'

'No. I'm Dicky. That's my name.'

'Ah. On the same page. Good ticket, Dicky.'

'Otherwise known as Viscount Washbourne . . . and my life is in danger.'

'Oh, so there *is* something wrong with you? Heart dicky, Dicky?'

'No. There are people who want to kill me.'

'The stenchers! Why in the name of strawberries would they want to do that?'

'Because I have a secret that they want to remain a secret.'

'Well, fair biddles to both of you,' said Blotto.

'Sorry?' asked Viscount Washbourne.

Blotto thought it rather strange that he needed to explain his reasoning. But maybe the poor pineapple was a widge deficient in the grey cell department. Bit outside the rule book to call attention to that in a boddo. 'You've got a secret, which when I was back at Eton, meant something you don't want anyone to know about . . . ?'

'Ye-es.'

'And the people you refer to as "they" don't want anyone to know about it either . . . ?'

'No-o.'

'So, you're both batting on the same team! And everything's creamy éclair!'

'Erm . . . Not quite,' said the young man. 'The fact is, they want my secret to die with me.'

'Well, that's no skin off your rice pudding, is it?'

'What do you mean?'

'The boddoes you're worried about aren't in a hurry, are they? If they're happy to wait till you shuffle off the mortals for your secret to die, then *nada problemo*. You're a young greengage, got lots of breathing time ahead of you.'

'I'm worried they want to cut down that breathing time.'

'How?' Blotto looked at the young man and the anguish furrowed into his brow brought enlightenment. 'You mean the lumps of toadspawn want to coffinate you?'

'Exactly that.'

'And in that way keep your secret secret?'

'Yes.'

'So, these boddoes, the ones you're up against, do you think they're capable of coffination?'

'They're capable of much worse. There is no evil they're not capable of.'

'Toad-in-the-hole!'

'What I'm up against is ... the Crooked Hand. Do you know what I mean by that?'

'I certainly do, by Denzil. I've been forced to play that murdy game of bridge with enough iffy stodgers to recognise the expression.'

'Well, the Crooked Hand are out to murder me.'

'Tough Gorgonzola, Dicky,' said Blotto. 'And have the stenchers got connections here at Clusters?'

'They certainly have. They're hand-in-glove with the people who've organised this weekend.'

'Well, I'll be kippered like a herring!' Blotto rubbed his chin thoughtfully. 'That is a bit of a chock in the cogwheel, isn't it?'

'You could say that.'

'I just did,' Blotto pointed out.

'Listen!' With sudden urgency, Viscount Washbourne reached into the inner pocket of his dinner suit. 'If you have this, then, even if they get me, they won't get the secret. Don't let anyone see it!'

And he thrust a stuffed envelope into his fellow diner's hands. Before Blotto had time to say anything, Viscount

Washbourne had left the table and was hurrying out of the Great Hall.

As his head turned, Blotto found himself staring deeply into the eyes of the Earl of Woking's unmarried daughter.

'Gosh,' she simpered. 'You are just so good-looking.'

'Don't talk such toffee,' said Blotto, as he thrust the envelope into the interior pocket of his evening wear.

It was the view of both Blotto and Twinks that the general sound level towards the end of the evening was most unseemly. Not that they were strangers to noisy dinners. Many a time, after a day's hunting, the raucous braying of their guests at Tawcester Towers had become totally incomprehensible (not that any of them had been much more comprehensible when they were sober). And a good few of Blotto's all-male dinners had ended up in food fights, with bread rolls being hurled at portraits of Lyminsters long dead.

But those had been jolly japes and larks perpetrated by their own sort. Perfectly acceptable in aristocratic circles. The rowdiness among the guests at Clusters that evening was of a completely different class (in every sense of the word). The noise raised by the Earl of Woking's assemblage of the dregs of society – accountants, solicitors, and linoleum salesmen – featured some truly terrible vowels. In fact, it sounded to Blotto and Twinks like the cacophony of a cattle market (not that either of them had ever visited so degraded a location).

They wondered what further degeneration the evening could hold for them. And their curiosity was quickly satisfied. As soon as those on the top table had finished their dessert course, and after the Clusters butler had, with considerable difficulty, imposed silence on the rabble, the Earl of Woking rose to his feet. He then appalled Blotto and Twinks by hoping that his guests had enjoyed their dinners. (This was way beyond the barbed wire. Oikish

34

sponge-worms like the line-up currently seated at the Earl's table should, in such surroundings, just be grateful for what they got. Whether they enjoyed it or not was totally immaterial.)

Then the Earl of Woking introduced his Master of the Revels.

'My Lords, ladies and gentlemen . . .' Mr Diamond began.

Blotto and Twinks caught each other's eyes. The majority of people in the Great Hall did not fit into any of those categories.

The aristocratic siblings were thunderstruck, however, by the Master of the Revels's next words. 'Let me tell you about the entertainments for the rest of the evening. For your further delectation,' the Master of the Revels continued, 'we have laid on three alternatives.'

Twinks winced, as she often did at such solecisms. 'Alternative', as everyone should know, came from the Latin '*alter*', meaning 'the other (of two)'. It was therefore semantically impossible, in any circumstances, to have more than two alternatives. How she suffered in the midst of such ignorance!

'For the more old-fashioned of you,' Mr Diamond went on, 'the billiards room is open, and tables for bridge are laid out in the Lesser Library.'

Old-fashioned? Blotto almost snorted out loud. Billiards and bridge were all that need ever be offered after dinner during a country house weekend party. Yes, bridge was indescribably dull, and billiards had long ago lost their lustre for Blotto because he always beat everyone so easily (particularly when they had been wobbulated by the best of the Tawcester Towers cellar). But it was inappropriate to offer any entertainments other than billiards and bridge. A stately home was not a seaside funfair.

Mr Diamond's sacrilege continued. 'For those of you who wish to trip the light fantastic, to turn a toe in the Charleston or Black Bottom . . .' Boisterous and unseemly

35

cheers from the younger diners greeted this suggestion '. . . the jazz band will continue to play in the Main Library.' More intemperate cheers.

'And for those of you who are interested in . . .' The Master of the Revels dropped his voice to a sinister depth '. . . those you of whose sleep last night may have been disturbed by spectral visitations, there will be, in the Lower Hall, an opportunity to make contact with the Other Side, in the presence of the renowned medium, Signora Zucchini.'

Neither Blotto nor Twinks had ever heard the name, but the reaction from the evening-dressed riff-raff around them indicated that they were in the minority. Signora Zucchini was the attraction which most of those present wanted to see. Chairs were pushed back – in many cases knocked over – in the scramble of guests on their way to the Lower Hall.

Blotto met his sister in the crush by the main doors. 'What say, Twinks me old can of pineapple chunks – shall we rouse Corky and pongle straight back to T.T.?'

'Not on a tin tray on the Cresta Run!' said Twinks.

'Sorry? I'm on a different page . . . ?'

'I came here, Blotters, convinced there was some thimble-jiggling going on. And I'm not going to leave Clusters until I've identified who's been playing the diddler's hand.'

'Tickey-tockey,' said Blotto. 'If you say so.' Which is what he always said when his sister told him to do something.

As they were swept along on the tide of people towards the Lower Hall, they heard an excited voice, with a distinct costermonger's twang, say, 'Certainly getting our money's worth, aren't we?'

Blotto and Twinks shared identical shudders.

6

Visitations

'I am extremely sensitive to the aura of buildings,' trilled Signora Zucchini. Her voice was heavily accented, high, birdlike.

Inside the Lower Hall, whose panelled walls were hung with portraits of former Earls of Woking and their families, the crowd was as silent now as it had been noisy in getting there. Their rapt attention was focused on the tiny figure on stage, dwarfed by the throne-like chair she perched on. There was a table beside her, on which stood a squat white candle, whose flame, wavering uneasily in spectral draughts, provided the cavernous room's only source of light.

Quite what the medium's face or body shape looked like it was hard to say. She was swathed in layers of black lace. From a black toque hat descended a veil which shrouded the pallor of her face.

'Buildings,' she went on, 'are not only places in which we live, they are also witnesses to our lives. They see everything that we do. They do not comment but they remember. The stones of an ancient building like Clusters contain many memories.'

Blotto and Twinks exchanged looks. Mutual under-standing, from the nursery onwards, meant that they did not need words to express the thoughts they shared. Which in this case were: 'Ancient'? Call a place that's not been up much more than four hundred years 'ancient'? If you want to see the real Best in Show, clap your peepers on Tawcester Towers!

'These stones,' Signora Zucchini intoned, 'have witnessed love affairs, betrayals, conspiracies and murders. I could sense that crushing weight of history when I first crossed the threshold of Clusters. The stones speak to me, the stones speak through me. And I am here to interpret their messages, to reveal to you what history is dying – or, more literally, has died – to tell you.'

A shiver ran through her tiny frame. 'Already, I can feel the dead wishing to speak to me. Wishing to speak to you through me. I can hear their voices, many, many voices. At the moment, they are just a jumble of sounds, but soon they will separate and individual voices will tell me what they wish to communicate. And who they wish to communicate to.'

She took a long, self-indulgent pause before asking, 'Are you ready to hear those voices?'

There was a murmur of avid assent from the gathered guests.

'I demand,' said Signora Zucchini, 'complete silence from you all while I make contact with the Other Side.'

Her wish was obeyed. In the Lower Hall hardly a breath was taken, as the diminutive figure onstage went through a series of bodily contortions. After a moment of total stillness, something like an electric shock juddered through her tiny form. Then, one after the other, her arms lifted into the air and waved about in a passable impression of anchored seaweed. They circled, as if tracing a halo around her head, and dropped to her lap, too heavy to be supported. Her whole body slumped, as if all her muscles had been replaced by soggy spaghetti.

'She's as crooked as a three-dollar note,' Twinks murmured to her brother.

This prompted furious local hissing for her to keep quiet. Everyone else believed themselves to be in the presence of a genius with paranormal powers.

All at once, Signora Zucchini sat bolt upright and started to speak again. But her voice had changed completely. The fluting Italian accent had been replaced by a patrician English masculine rumble.

With the change of voice came another manifestation. A light, whose flickering source was invisible, suddenly illuminated a portrait of the fifth Earl of Woking, wearing the voluminous wig of the Restoration period. And, as Signora Zucchini spoke, the painted lips moved in time to her words!

A communal gasp arose from the audience, quickly followed by silence as they listened to the medium's – or the Earl's – revelations.

'Welcome to Clusters,' the voice boomed. 'Here is history come to life. Here you can enjoy the benefits of the wisdom of the ages. You have passed through the door which leads to the Other Side. We, the dead, may just be shadows, but we are shadows with much shared experience. Any question you put to us, we will be able to provide the answer. And if you wish to contact anyone on the Other Side, ask and it shall be given unto you! I, the fifth Earl of Woking, will provide the information you require. Say, is there anyone here at Clusters tonight who wishes to seek help from the accumulated wisdom of the dead?'

At this, there was much confused mumbling from the audience, until one strong male voice emerged. 'I wish to contact one of the dead,' it cried sonorously.

'That is possible,' came the reply. The audience had by now forgotten the small, black-clad figure from whom the voice emanated. Their attention was fixed on the moving lips of the fifth Earl of Woking. 'Who is it you wish to contact?' he asked.

'It is my butler, Hargreaves,' came the reply from the depths of the Lower Hall. 'Two weeks ago, having helped himself to too much of my 1887 Taylor's Port, Hargreaves smashed my Hispano-Suiza into a tree. An oak, actually. Apart from the extensive damage to the car, his death caused me other nuisances. And I wish to ask Hargreaves something that would considerably ease my current predicament. Could you bring him up from the Other Side?'

'I will endeavour to do so,' said the painted lips. 'It should not be too difficult. The recently dead tend to hang around the reception area for some time, finding their feet, as it were . . . or perhaps coming to terms with the fact that they no longer have any feet. Give me a moment.'

The lips closed. The light that illuminated the portrait grew less strong. From Signora Zucchini's small body there emanated a series of deep sighs. These were the only sounds, until she suddenly jerked awake and spoke again in the fifth Earl's voice. 'I have found your man Hargreaves. If you are hoping to get from him an apology for what happened to your Hispano-Suiza, I am afraid he does not seem to be in a mood which would make him likely to provide one.'

'Never mind that,' said the questioner. 'All I want to know is where he put the bloody key to the wine cellar!'

A ripple of laughter greeted this deeply practical enquiry, and it grew as the sanctimonious voice of a butler emanated from Signora Zucchini, saying, 'It's on top of the cupboard in my pantry.'

'He's a plant,' Twinks hissed to her brother.

'Who is?'

'The one who asked the spoffing question.'

'Is he?' Blotto peered through the gloom. 'He doesn't look like one.' He reconsidered this assessment. 'Well, maybe a bit like an aspidistra.'

Twinks had been through too many comparable mis-understandings with her brother to pass any comment.

As the laughter subsided, the voice from the medium reverted to that of the fifth Earl, and the portrait's lips moved as the next question was posed. 'Is there anyone else who requires information from the Other Side?'

'Yes,' said a voice which Twinks recognised as that of the money bore who had been seated next to her at dinner. 'Are there any financial experts on the Other Side?'

'Of course,' came the reply from the fifth Earl. 'There is every kind of expert on the Other Side. If you think of the number of people who have died over the centuries, then we have here an expert in any subject you might wish to ask about.'

'Good,' said the money bore. 'So, can you find me an expert on the current state of the British Stock Market?'

'No sooner requested than done,' the portrait replied. 'I have with me a phenomenally successful investor who died only last week. And, of course, because he is now on the Other Side, he can not only see how stocks have performed in the past, but also see how they will fare in the future.'

'Excellent!' said the questioner. 'Just the kind of chap I need. So, will you ask him ... should I sell my considerable number of shares in British Amalgamated Screws? They have been outperforming many other stocks in recent months and look set fair to continue that upwards trend. What does your recently deceased investor say I should do? Buy more of the stock?'

'No,' boomed the fifth Earl. 'He advises that you should sell immediately.'

'What? But screws are essential to the construction industry and there is a building boom on at the moment.'

'That may be so, says the investor, but he can see into the future. Already, in an engineer's workshop in Warminster, is being developed a universal rivet which will replace the screw in all building projects. The value of British Amalgamated Screws has gone as high as it will ever go. Get out before the crash! Sell, sell, sell!'

'Thank you,' said the money bore. 'I will do that.'

'And, Earl,' asked another eager, acquisitive voice, 'is there any newer stock which your investor would recommend, something that's cheap at the moment but whose value is about to soar a hundredfold?'

'I will consult him,' said the fifth Earl. There was a long tense silence to allow time for a presumed consultation. Then came the confident reply, 'Sell everything you've got and put it all into a small company called Aristotours!'

This pronouncement was followed by a rustle of mingled surprise and approval.

'The four-faced filchers!' Twinks hissed to her brother.

'What are the stenchers doing?' asked Blotto.

'I'd put my last shred of laddered silk stocking on the fact that Aristotours is the company running this whole three-ring circus. They're only trying to inflate the price of their own shares!'

'Oh. Tickey-tockey,' said Blotto. It was his favoured response when he didn't understand something.

'Any other questions?' demanded the fifth Earl of Woking.

The voice which responded from the audience was female, tremulous, almost frightened. But also with a twang that told Blotto and Twinks that its owner hadn't been to the right schools. 'Some of us who spent last night here at Clusters were woken by strange visitations.'

'I apologise for my relations,' said the portrait. 'Curiosity is the besetting sin of the whole family. They were aware of strangers in their ancestral hall and merely wished to identify who you were.'

'Oh,' said the woman who wasn't quite the genuine article, before asking fearfully, 'and are such manifestations likely to appear again tonight?'

'Very likely,' said the fifth Earl. His words were rewarded by a delighted communal *frisson* from the audience. They loved the idea of being haunted. 'Saturday is the night that we from the Other Side traditionally let our hair down. Or in some cases,' he said with a spectral chuckle, 'let our heads down.'

Signora Zucchini suddenly reverted to her own fluttery tones. 'I am sorry. My strength is fading. The effort of maintaining contact with the Other Side is too powerful for a frail living body. I can ask one last question of the fifth Earl and then the session will be at an end.'

The prompt was taken up instantly. 'At country house weekend parties, there is a tradition that a murder takes place. Is there going to be one at Clusters this weekend?'

'Undoubtedly,' replied the fifth Earl of Woking.

There was great excitement among the guests streaming out of the Lower Hall. The promise of ghostly visitations *and* a murder had exceeded their highest expectations. Blotto and Twinks only wished the oikish sponge-worms could have expressed their enthusiasm with better vowels.

Ready to follow the mob out of the doors at the back, Blotto was surprised to find himself been steered by his sister in the other direction, towards the now vacant stage where Signora Zucchini had sat. 'Want to see how the thimble-jiggling was done, Blotto me old trouser turn-up,' she murmured.

'Good ticket,' he said. Anything suggested by Twinks was a good ticket, as far as he was concerned.

She was now at the edge of the stage, peering up towards the portrait of the fifth Earl. 'Who in the name of strawberries made the lips move?'

'A ghost?' her brother hazarded.

'A ghost? Stuff that for a taxidermist's dummy! There's no such thing as a spoffing ghost. When people are coffin-ated, they stay coffinated. No, Blotters, there's definitely been some sneaky backdoor-sidling here.'

Unable to see what she was looking for, Twinks jumped up on the stage to get nearer the portrait. At that moment, two burly footmen appeared through a side door and took up positions between her and the back wall. 'I'm sorry. No one's allowed on the stage, miss.'

'I am not "miss",' announced Twinks, suddenly reincarnated into her mother. 'To the likes of you, I am "milady"!'

'I apologise, milady.' But neither footman moved.

'Look here, you lumps of toadspawn,' said Blotto boldly. 'If you don't shift your shimmies and let my sister through, you're likely to feel the knobbly side of my cricket bat.'

The footmen took up defensive postures, but Twinks got down from her high horse as quickly as she had mounted it. '*Nada problemo*, Blotters,' she said. 'Let us pongle off on our own sweet way.'

Puzzled, but knowing she had her reasons, Blotto meekly followed his sister out of a side door. As they departed, the two footmen started removing the huge chair and table from the stage.

'We've got to be as quick as cheetahs on spikes,' Twinks hissed at her brother. 'While those two are busy, we can get round the back and find evidence of how that leadpenny medium sleeved the cards. I'll point my peepers through this door. You skiddle through that one.'

Blotto was through the door before he realised that he hadn't asked what he was meant to be looking for.

In her searches, Twinks was quickly rewarded. The door through which she had passed led to a dimly lit corridor, running directly behind the back wall of the Lower Hall. A stepladder stood to one side, beneath a small shelf, on which was an electric torch.

When she switched this on, a treasure trove of equipment was revealed. Wires ran from a large wet-cell battery through holes in the wall. Presumably, that powered the light that had flickered round the portrait on the other side.

A small circle had been cut into the wall on the Lower Hall side and covered with gauze. Twinks quickly deduced that it must have been lined up with the mouth on the fifth Earl's portrait and painted over.

Then there was a device like a child's toy of clacking false teeth, which could be opened and closed by hand. On to this rubber lips had been affixed. When Twinks turned the torchlight on them, they glowed, pinkly luminous. So that was how the crowd in the Lower Hall had witnessed the fifth Earl speaking!

Twinks's last remaining question – how did the operator in the corridor synchronise the lip movement with what Signora Zucchini said? – was quickly answered. Also on the shelf was a typewritten script. As she scanned it under the torch beam, Twinks saw all of the dialogue mapped out.

The questions which came, apparently spontaneously, from the audience had been scripted. The people who'd asked them were all plants, part of the conspiracy to convince people that Signora Zucchini had special powers.

Twinks felt extremely pleased with the success of her investigation. She murmured to herself the cry of triumph, 'Larksissimo!'

Blotto's discovery was not so triumphant, but equally surprising.

The door he had passed through did not lead to a corridor, but a dimly lit spiral staircase. He mounted the stone steps, his empty brain still rattling with the question of what he was meant to be looking for. This did not worry him. Unless it was a matter of hunting (when it was a fox), he rarely knew what he was looking for.

There was no exit from the staircase until he reached the top, about the height of two storeys. He found himself in a small room like a study. Pale moonlight trickled through the leaded panes. The only other illumination came from two candles on a desk.

Their brass sticks stood at either side of something in the middle.

The something was the body of Viscount Washbourne, lying face downwards. Out of the back of his dinner jacket protruded a knife.

The name etched in false silver on the false ivory handle was: 'Lord Devereux Lyminster'.

7

An Arrest

Blotto's first reaction was to say, 'Well, I'll be jugged like a hare!' It was that serious.

Then he reached forward, wondering whether pulling the knife out of the dead man's back would help. It felt pretty firmly embedded, so he left it there, rubbing his hand against his trousers to wipe off the worst of the blood.

Before he had time to think what he should do next, another door opened to admit the Earl of Woking, his Master of the Revels and Baron Chipping Norton.

'Good heavens!' cried the Earl. 'What's going on here?'

'It is a bit of a treacle tin,' said Blotto. 'This poor old thimble seems to have tumbled off the trailer.'

'A corpse? At Clusters?' said the Earl.

'Yes, bit of a rum baba,' Blotto sympathised. 'About as welcome to you as a slug in a shower, I dare say. And it doesn't look like an accident. I'm afraid someone bought the poor droplet's one-way ticket to the Pearlies for him.'

'"Someone"?' asked Baron Chipping Norton sharply.

'Well, yes.' Patiently, Blotto explained. Apparently, he was up against one of those few people in the world who was less intellectually gifted than he was. 'You see, Baron me old toothpick, this boddo couldn't have done it to himself, you know, slipped the slicer between his own shoulder blades. The old arms couldn't reach that far.

47

I mean, even if the poor greengage was one of those pineapples in the circus who can tie themselves in reef knots – you know, a controversialist – he still couldn't have done it. So, some other stencher must have done it for him.'

He thought that covered most of the bases.

'That was exactly my point,' said the Baron icily. 'He was murdered.'

'Give that pony a rosette!' said Blotto. 'Fizzulated that we're on the same page.'

'Sorry,' said the Earl, 'but who is it?'

'Who's who?' asked Blotto.

'The corpse. The victim. I don't recognise him from his back-view.'

'Oh. Tickey-tockey,' said Blotto. 'Poor thimble was sitting next to me at nosebags. Hadn't met him before that. Goes under the name-tag of Viscount Washbourne.'

'And you say you hadn't met him before?' demanded Baron Chipping Norton.

'You're bong on the nose there. Never met a Viscount Washbourne in all my bornies.'

'That's a lie.'

'Now rein in the roans there,' said Blotto, rather affronted. 'I know whether I know boddoes or not.'

'Viscount Washbourne was your exact contemporary at Eton.'

'Not on your nuthatch, Baron! None of my old muffin-toasters was called "Washbourne".'

'He wasn't called "Washbourne" then. It was later that he inherited the title. At Eton he was known as Nigel Wickerstaff.'

'Scrub out the "Nigel". At Eton none of the boddoes had a Christian name.'

'"Wickerstaff" then,' the Baron insisted. 'Surely you'd remember being an exact contemporary of someone called "Wickerstaff"?'

'Doesn't blip the brain cells, no.' Blotto had an idea. 'Just a momentette . . .'

'What?'

'This Wickerstaff boddo – did he play cricket?'

'No. He suffered from asthma.'

Blotto spread his hands wide. 'Well, there you are then. That straightens the corkscrew. If the poor little thimble didn't play cricket, then of course I didn't know him.'

'Hm,' the Baron grunted sardonically. 'You expect me to believe that?'

'No skin off my rice pudding whether you do or don't. But I can't see why it spoffing well matters whether I knew the boddo or not.'

'Can't you? If you did know him in the past, then there could well have been bad blood between you for a long time.'

'"Bad blood"? Why in the name of ginger should there be bad blood between us?'

'I don't know. But the motives for crimes often go back a long way.'

'"Motives for crimes"? What are you on about? Come on, uncage the ferrets.'

'Viscount Washbourne is undoubtedly dead . . .' Baron Chipping Norton began frigidly.

'You've popped the partridge there, old chum.'

'And the knife that killed him has your name on it.'

'Yes. Rather nasty little flipmadoodles, aren't they? Bad enough not to possess any family silver in the first place, but these little wodjermabits just draw attention to the fact.'

'We do have family silver,' protested an incensed Earl of Woking.

'Tickey-tockey,' said Blotto. 'Then why don't we use it?'

'This dinner was a special occasion.'

The Master of the Revels came in to support his employer. 'The personalised cutlery was my idea,' he said, as frigid as the Baron.

'Oh, tough Gorgonzola,' Blotto sympathised. 'You can't win a coconut every time, can you?'

'Could we get back to the matter in hand!' bellowed Baron Chipping Norton. 'Lord Lyminster, Viscount Washbourne was killed by your knife. Which might well turn out to have your fingerprints on it. And there is blood on your hands.'

'Yes, but don't get the wrong end of the sink plunger.'

'Also, you're pretending not to know someone you spent many years at school with.'

'Yes, but I've untangled the plait on that one. Boddo didn't play cricket, so I never met the poor pineapple.'

'That sounds a pretty feeble story to me.' The Baron pressed his case. 'Wouldn't stand up in court.'

'"Court"? Why are you cluntering on about "court"?'

'Because court is where murderers usually end up, Lord Lyminster!'

'Just a momentette, Baron! Don't bash before the bully-off. Are you suggesting that I coffinated the Viscount?'

'It very much looks that way.'

'But why in the name of snitchrags would I want to do a thing like that?'

The Baron had his answer ready for that one. 'Because Viscount Washbourne was in possession of a secret, so valuable that you thought it worth killing him to steal it.'

'Don't talk such meringue.'

The word 'secret' had, however, prompted an uncomfortable memory in Blotto, and he wasn't totally surprised when the Baron asked, 'What is making that large bulge in the inside pocket of your jacket?'

Blotto produced the stuffed envelope. 'It's just—'

Before he had time to say more, the Baron had appropriated the envelope and looked at its contents. Blotto saw a sheaf of papers, headed 'Aristotours', before it was whisked out of sight. He wondered what the documents were. Viscount Washbourne's secret, perhaps? A secret that it was worth committing murder for?

Baron Chipping Norton turned a beady eye on him. 'Do you deny that you got that package from Viscount Washbourne?'

'Erm . . . no,' said Blotto wretchedly.

The Baron turned to the Earl of Woking. 'Call the police! Tell them there has been a murder at Clusters. And we have found the perpetrator!'

8

To the Rescue!

The Tawcestershire Constabulary was represented by two officers, Chief Inspector Trumbull and Sergeant Knatchbull, who operated out of Tawsworthy police station. As well as their normal duties, because Tawcestershire was a county which contained more than its fair share of stately homes, they were constantly being summoned to murders which had taken place during country house weekend parties.

It was an occupational hazard, and the two men knew well what their role in the proceedings would be. They would attend the scene of the crime, miss obvious clues, reach wrong conclusions, and declare themselves to be baffled. They would remain baffled while they waited stoically for some polymathic amateur sleuth, who conveniently happened to be one of the weekend guests, to solve the crime. The polymathic amateur sleuth would then ask all the guests to assemble in the library where, after an extremely long exoneration of the other suspects, he would point a finger at the perpetrator.

The perpetrator would be handed across to Trumbull and Knatchbull, who would incarcerate him or her in the prison cell in Tawsworthy police station and set in motion the official legal processes which would take the accused to remand prison and, ultimately, to trial. The investigation would then be concluded tidily on the gallows. The death sentence was, in the view of the two policemen and a long list of amateur sleuths, a highly convenient way of ensuring there were no loose ends after a murder investigation.

So, when they got the call from the Earl of Woking late on the Saturday evening, saying there had been a murder whose perpetrator had been apprehended, Chief Inspector Trumbull and Sergeant Knatchbull knew exactly the routine they had to follow.

Blotto did think it rather tiresome that he had to go to Tawsworthy police station, but no more than tiresome. The situation was not complicated. Mistakes had been made and the over-zealous Baron of Chipping Norton had gone shinnying up the wrong drainpipe. That was all that had happened. The misunderstanding could be sorted out as quick as a lizard's lick. And Blotto would be able to take his place the next morning on the Tawcester Towers cricket pitch to face the might of the Marquis of Hartlepool's Irrelevancies.

Blotto had great faith in the efficacy and majesty of British justice.

And he didn't know that there were some four-faced filchers involved in his current predicament whose sole aim was to pervert the course of that majestic British justice.

Twinks was pretty vinegared off as Corky Froggett drove her back alone in the Rolls-Royce to Tawcester Towers. Excited by her own discovery about the charlatanism of Signora Zucchini, she had arrived rather late on the scene of Viscount Washbourne's murder. In fact, she had arrived after her brother had been driven off in a Black Maria to Tawsworthy police station.

'This really is the flea's armpit,' she complained disconsolately to Corky. 'Blotters has been stitched up like a moccasin. He's not the kind of boddo to go round coffinating people.'

'I am fully aware of that, milady,' the chauffeur concurred.

'They set him up like a row of skittles.'

'Have you any idea why they might want to do that, milady?'

'Not a mouse-squeak of one,' Twinks confessed. 'But I'll straighten the corkscrew. Just give me a momentette.'

Corky shared her confidence in her intellect. The young mistress could always work things out.

'And do you know what's the real stye in the eye on this one, Corky?'

'No, milady.'

'With Blotto jugged up like a hare, I can't question him about the murder. Apparently, he was first on the S of the C. So, he undoubtedly has vital information about how the poor droplet was coffinated and I can't ask him about it.'

'A frustrating situation, milady.'

'You can say that with two cherries on, Corky. Do you know, the stenchers wouldn't even let me in to cast my peepers over the S of the C?'

'Which stenchers would these be, milady?'

'Well, it was the Earl of Woking who refused me the admission ticket, but I think the other two were playing him like a cat's cradle.'

'"Other two", milady?'

'Mr Diamond, the slugbucket Woking introduces as his Master of the Revels, and another filcher who's recently purchased the barony of Chipping Norton.'

'I'm afraid I did not meet either of the gentlemen.'

'"Gentlemen" is rather dressing up snails as lobster, Corky.'

'Sorry, milady. The two "men", perhaps?'

'Better. Still over-generous. Anyway, there's definitely been some sneaky backdoor-sidling going on.' Twinks sighed mournfully. 'It's a real candle-snuffer, being so near to a murder and not being able to focus the microscope on it. I wish Blotters could somehow get out of that clinkbox!'

Corky Froggett didn't state his intentions out loud, but from that moment he was determined to fulfil the young mistress's wish.

Having deposited Twinks at the main doors, the chauffeur drove the Rolls-Royce back to the Tawcester Towers garages. Then, rather than retiring to his quarters, he went to his workshop and picked up his toolbox, along with some ropes and other miscellaneous objects. From another garage, he got out the young master's pride and joy, his gleaming blue Lagonda. Deliberately not switching on the headlights, the chauffeur drove cautiously towards the Tawcestershire's county town, Tawsworthy.

On the way, Corky Froggett made his plans. None of his training during 'the recent dust-up against the Hun' would be wasted. He was a highly tuned killing machine and, though he did not anticipate any actual killing being involved in his current mission, he'd be ready for it if the need arose. Once again, he mentally bemoaned the efficacy of the 1918 Armistice. Though he was confident there would be another global war at some point, he worried that, when it did happen, he might be too old to enjoy it.

Though the head office of the Tawcestershire Constabulary, Tawsworthy police station was not a large or prepossessing building. Nor did it need to be. The kind of crimes dealt with there were usually issues of poaching (particularly from the Tawcester Towers estate), inebriation (particularly on market days) and petty thieving (particularly the appropriation of underwear from washing lines).

55

So, despite the number of stately homes in the county, it was rare for the station to provide accommodation for a suspected murderer.

It was even rarer for it to provide accommodation for a member of the aristocracy. Chief Inspector Trumbull apologised to Blotto as he showed him his cell, and actually sent Sergeant Knatchbull off to fetch clean towels from his home. Their prisoner, who had been in much worse lockups, most recently – and steamily – in the Palace of the Maharajah of Koorbleimee, was not too bothered by where he was staying. It was the fact that he was away from Tawcester Towers that put lumps in his custard.

More importantly, he was meant to be playing in a cricket match the following day.

He tried again and again to make this point to Trumbull and Knatchbull, but without success. They stuck to their – to Blotto's mind, rather old-fashioned – view that, in terms of social commitments, being arrested for murder was more important than a cricket match. Even when it was a matter of revenge against the Marquis of Hartlepool's Irrelevancies? he asked. They remained unpersuaded. Sometimes Blotto despaired of the lower classes.

But then, the final word he had from Chief Inspector Trumbull rather changed his mind about the situation. 'You need not worry, milord,' said the officer. 'If you are innocent—'

'Which I spoffing well am!'

'. . . then you need have no fear. When you have gone through the relevant legal processes, you, milord, will not be found guilty of a crime you did not commit. And therein lies the majesty of British justice.'

Blotto found it surprisingly comforting to hear that from such an unlikely source. At least there was one point on which he and the Chief Inspector agreed.

Further conversation was halted by the departure of the two officers, and the prisoner settled down on to the hard bed of his cell. Fortunately, he'd drunk enough at the

Clusters dinner to slip easily into the untroubled sleep of the innocent.

Given the importance of the prisoner who was enjoying the hospitality of Tawsworthy police station, neither Chief Inspector Trumbull nor Sergeant Knatchbull were going to leave their posts that night. There was a bedroom upstairs for just such occasions, and rank dictated that the Chief Inspector should claim it for himself. Sergeant Knatchbull was deputed to stay in the office downstairs to guard the prisoner. The cells were in the basement of the building, with no windows, just air vents at ground level. No one could escape without passing through the office.

Chief Inspector Trumbull had not said whether he required his junior to stay awake while on guard duty, and Sergeant Knatchbull reckoned it was already long past his bedtime. So, after putting the cell keys down on the office desk, he allowed his head to join them. And he was soon sleeping as innocently as his prisoner.

Being innocent, both men dreamed innocent dreams. Blotto was carrying his bat on the cricket field, proud of the double century he had just scored against the Marquis of Hartlepool's Irrelevancies. Knatchbull, on the other hand, was dreaming of being presented with a carriage clock at the small ceremony celebrating the end of his career in the Tawcestershire Constabulary.

Each was in his own private heaven.

Corky Froggett parked the Lagonda, lights still off, in the market square of Tawsworthy, some distance from the police station. He didn't want his approach to be heard by the officers inside. Taking the relevant tools, ropes, and other equipment from the dickey, he walked noiselessly towards his target.

His experiences behind enemy lines during 'the recent dust-up' had taught him many lessons, one of the most important of which was: if a building only has one entrance, that is the one that's going to be guarded.

As a result, he didn't even bother to look at the front door of Tawsworthy police station. Though, amongst his kit, he had a lockpick that would open it, going in that way was guaranteed to alert and provoke resistance from the policemen inside. No, Corky Froggett was too canny an operator to be caught in such an obvious trap.

He decided to use as a model the break-in he had masterminded in 1917 to the German High Command, temporarily housed in the *mairie* of Vaundry-Courdelion. His commanding officer had tasked Corky with a midnight mission to cross No Man's Land on his own, make his way through the German trenches to the town and steal from the *mairie* some top-secret maps which would reveal the enemy's next plan of attack.

He was pleased to see that, like the *mairie* at Vaundry-Courdelion, Tawsworthy police station had an unlit lamppost standing beside it. It was a matter of moments for Corky, careless of any possible damage to his chauffeur's uniform, to shin up to the top and attach one of his ropes firmly to the crossbeam just below the lantern.

Moustache bristling in the thin moonlight, he gripped the rope tightly in both hands and swung across the void to land neatly on the sloping tiles of the police station roof. Attaching himself securely by another rope to the chimney, Corky Froggett took out of his pocket a pair of carpenter's pincers and started to remove the wooden pegs which held the tiles in place.

It took him the best part of an hour before he had made a hole in the roof wide enough for him to slip through. Holding on to his rope, Corky lowered himself gently into the void, his feet feeling for the rafters. He thought it unlikely that the police station's loft would be boarded in, and so it proved. Were he to tread on anything but the rafters, he would have fallen through into the bedroom currently occupied by Chief Inspector Trumbull, whose snores through the ceiling had pinpointed exactly where he lay.

Using an electric torch, Corky Froggett edged along the rafters until he found a hatch which opened down on to the bathroom adjacent to the bedroom. Attaching a rope ladder he had brought with him to the diagonal rafters, he lowered himself silently to the floor, then edged on to the landing. Trumbull's snores continued uninterrupted.

As Corky tiptoed down the stairs to the ground floor, the rhythm of the snores from above was augmented by a descant from below. This warned the intruder, since he was convinced (wrongly) that the young master didn't do anything as *déclassé* as to snore, that there was a second guard on the ground floor.

Corky peered into the office. Seeing the cell keys on the desk, he lifted them soundlessly, causing no break in the rhythm of Sergeant Knatchbull's snores. He then went down to the basement.

Having unlocked the cell door, he was surprised how long it took him to wake the young master. Finally coherent enough to recognise his faithful chauffeur, Blotto asked, 'What in the name of snitchrags are you doing here, Corky?'

'I have come to rescue you, milord.'

'Rescue me from what?'

'Have you not noticed, milord? You are in the cells of Tawsworthy police station.'

'Tickey-tockey. That had blipped on the brain cells, yes.'

'And I have come to rescue you from durance vile.'

'What, you mean – you're going to spring me like a bed-spring?'

'Exactly so, milord. And then drive you in the Lag back to Tawcester Towers. Thus enabling you to take part tomorrow in the cricket match against the Marquis of Hartlepool's Irrelevancies.'

Blotto shook his head. 'Not on the menu, I'm afraid, Corky.'

'What do you mean, milord?'

'If I were to leave this fumacious cell before I have gone through the relevant legal processes, then I would be offering a resounding snubbins to the majesty of British justice. And that would be way beyond the barbed wire.'

'Are you saying, milord, that you are refusing to be rescued?'

'You're bong on the nose there, Corky.'

'Even if it means missing the match against the Marquis of Hartlepool's Irrelevancies?'

'Give that pony another rosette!'

Corky Froggett felt disconsolate. There were times when it was exceedingly difficult dealing with someone whose sense of honour was as highly developed as the young master's.

The chauffeur's mood was not improved when, trying the front door of the police station before retracing his steps back to the roof, he found it had been unlocked all the time.

Then he remembered that his mission to the *mairie* of Vaundry-Courdelion had ended badly too. The maps he had stolen from the German High Command had been so valuable to the Allies that they had considerably shortened the duration of the war. When all Corky had wanted was for it to go on as long as possible, so that he would continue to have an excuse for killing people.

As soon as the Dowager Duchess was up on the Sunday morning, Twinks went to visit her in the Blue Morning Room. 'Mater,' she said, 'Blotto's jugged up like a hare in Tawsworthy police station.'

'Oh, what's the boy done this time?' the Dowager Duchess growled. 'Has he knocked another vicar off his bike with the Lagonda? Broken another greenhouse with a cricket ball when practising his cover drive? Stolen another policeman's helmet?'

'No, he's been accused of murder.'

'Oh, that's all right,' said the Dowager Duchess, considerably relieved.

'Well, Mater, can you get him out of this particular treacle tin?'

'Yes, of course, Twinks. Leave it with me.'

Tawcester Towers only boasted one telephone and that was situated in the cavernous and chilly hall. So, when she needed to make a call, even the Dowager Duchess had to go down there. Usually, such communications were with what she called her 'friends', lesser female aristocrats with shorter bloodlines, whom she took great relish in patronising. Her manner at such times was loud and bullying. (Indeed, the butler Grimshaw had been heard to question whether, given the volume of her voice into the receiver, she actually needed the intervention of a telephone to make herself heard throughout the county of Tawcestershire.)

'This is the Chief Constable's office,' said the answering secretarial voice.

'Put him through!' the Dowager Duchess bellowed.

'I'm afraid Mr Anstruther is in a meeting with the Head of Scotland Yard and—'

'Put Bertie on the line!'

There are some voices which demand to be heard and the secretary knew she was hearing one of them. 'Who shall I say is speaking?' she asked timorously.

'The Dowager Duchess of Tawcester!' announced the Dowager Duchess of Tawcester . . . unsurprisingly, really, because that's who she was.

The line went almost silent for a moment, there was some muttered conversation, then the Chief Constable, sounding more confident than he felt, was on the line. 'Your Grace, how may I help you?'

'Blotto's being held in Tawsworthy police station. Get him out of there! And get him back to Tawcester Towers by eleven! He is playing in an important cricket match.'

'May I ask, Your Grace, why he is being held in Tawsworthy police station?'

'He's been charged with murder.'

'Oh? Do you know whether he's guilty or not guilty?'

'I don't give a tuppenny farthing whether he's guilty or not guilty. Get him back here in time for the cricket match!'

'I'm afraid, Your Grace, there are certain legal processes to—'

'I don't care about "legal processes", Bertie! Get Blotto out of that police station and back here by eleven . . .'

'Your Grace, I can't just—'

'Listen! You and Blotto were muffin-toasters together at Eton.'

'And friendship is important, I agree, Your Grace, but when it's a matter of murder—'

'I have known you since you were in short petticoats in the nursery. You have been our guest at Tawcester Towers on more than one occasion. And, Bertie, I'm sure you don't want me to raise the memory of a certain misjudgement on the part of your mother which might prompt investigations into your paternity . . .'

Blotto was back at Tawcester Towers in time for the match against the Marquis of Hartlepool's Irrelevancies. The charges against him hadn't been dropped, but the Chief Constable had agreed bail conditions with the Dowager Duchess. The main one being, that Blotto would not be allowed to leave Tawcester Towers, which would present no problem for him. Everything he required from life was readily available on the estate. And, although his adventures with Twinks had frequently taken him to foreign climes, like most true-born Englishmen, he basically hated 'abroad'.

The Dowager Duchess agreed with Sir Albert Anstruther that Blotto would attend Tawsworthy police station on the Monday morning for further questioning, but had no intention that her son would comply with further restrictions on his freedom.

So far as she was concerned, the case was over. And Blotto felt exactly the same way. He was off the hook.

9

The Professor of Everything

The dream Blotto had had in Tawsworthy police station proved to be remarkably prescient. He did score a double century in the home team's win over the Marquis of Hartlepool's Irrelevancies. (Sadly, Sergeant Knatchbull's dream could not be realised quite so quickly.) And the timing had been good. The game had been completed in warm September sunshine, just before the sky was filled with torrential rain.

The cricket match had prevented Blotto from communicating with his sister until later on the Sunday evening. Once again, they sat in her boudoir over steaming mugs of cocoa. Smoke from her cigarette spiralled lazily up from the silver and mother-of-pearl ashtray.

'Aristotours?' Twinks echoed the word her brother had just spoken.

'Yes, I'm certain that's what it said on the document. Blip any brain cells?'

His sister nodded her elegant head. 'Of course it does, Blotters. That was the name of the company we were told to invest in at Clusters. Remember?'

Blotto's less elegant – in fact, rather tousled – head was shaken. He didn't waste memory space on things he didn't understand.

'I'd put my last shred of silk stocking on the fact that they're up to something wooky. I'll do some rootling into the company's background and I'm sure I can come up with the right truffle.'

'Good ticket. When I was at Clusters, I very much got a whiff that something about the Stilton was iffy.'

'You've popped the partridge there, Blotters. For a start, that Signora Zucchini is about as genuine as a head-waiter's toupee.'

And Twinks told her brother about the apparatus she'd found in the corridor behind the fifth Earl's portrait. 'The script that was there,' she concluded, 'makes it pretty certain that all the boddoes who put the questionettes were . . .' about to say 'plants', she evaded further confusion by saying '. . . set-ups.'

'What I can't dab the digit on,' said Blotto, 'is why the four-faced filchers set me up as a coffinator. Apparently, I was at school with the victim, but I swear I'd never seen him before in my bornies.'

'I think they must have given him a one-way ticket to the Pearlies because they wanted to get hold of that fumacious envelope with the Aristotours papers in it. And someone must have seen him shuffle that across to you at the dinner table and thought that you were one of his co-conspirators.'

'Well, it's certainly a bit of a rum baba.' Blotto yawned. 'Anyway, after today's cricket and last night's hospitality with the Tawcestershire Constabulary, my peepers are in need of props. So, I'm going to wheel out the jim-jams.'

'Sleep as tight as a tick in the ticking,' said his sister fondly.

Twinks herself did not feel ready for sleep. She contemplated translating a bit more of *Three Men in a Boat* into the Mongolic Khalkha dialect, but couldn't get wildly excited about the prospect. There was something niggling at her.

And she knew she wouldn't have any peace until she had found out more about the mysterious 'Aristotours'.

It was after midnight. The rain was still pounding against the windows of Tawcester Towers. Twinks was dressed in her matching silk pyjamas and robe as she went down to the telephone in the hall. The rest of the great house was asleep, its silence broken only by the rain outside, the creaking of its ancient timbers settling down for the night and the creaking of the Dowager Duchess's ancient bones settling down for the night. All that was missing was the recurrent rumbling and clanking of the Tawcester Towers plumbing. That would have to wait until Rodney Perkins had finished his ministrations.

Twinks got through to the operator and gave the number of St Raphael's College, Oxford. Her call had evidently woken up the bleary night porter who answered. He struggled for politeness. St Raphael's was a college without undergraduates, a haven for elderly unmarried dons, indulging themselves in ever more arcane academic research and excellent High Table dinners.

'Could I speak to Professor Erasmus Holofernes?' asked Twinks.

The night porter was not surprised. If any of the residents of St Raphael's was going to receive a telephone call after midnight, then Holofernes was the most likely candidate. Not that he led an active social life. Except for dinners and the drinks in the Senior Common Room that preceded them, he rarely stirred from his profoundly cluttered rooms.

But he did have an amazing active life of research by correspondence and telephone. Basically, Professor Erasmus Holofernes knew everything. He was a giant sponge for information, which he gathered from academics and experts all over the world. As a result of his omniscience, he acted as a consultant to governments and individuals from every point of the moral compass (including some very dubious ones). The day porter at St Raphael's got used to putting through calls from monarchs and Mafia bosses. The night porter was not kept quite so busy, but he too was used to having his sleep disturbed by calls for the Professor. Rarely, though, was the voice at the other end of the line a woman's.

'My dear Twinks,' Holofernes's voice boomed, after the connection had been made. 'How enchanting to hear from you!'

'Sorry about the rather murdy hour of the night.'

'Do not concern yourself about that, my dear. I was still engaged in my studies. A White Russian prince is trying to track down a diamond necklace which he believes was buried by his mother in their estate at Vishni-Volgatov.'

'Oh well, Razzy, if I'm cracking into your ticking time . . .'

'Nonsense! Talking to you is always of paramount importance to me. There is nothing else on my desk.' The crashing sound which accompanied these words demonstrated that he had indeed swept all the papers off to join the Himalayas of documentation already obscuring his carpet. 'So . . . what can I do for you?'

'There is a word whose provenance I wish you to turn your truffler on.'

'And what is the word?'

'"Aristotours".'

'Hmm. It does not spark immediate recognition. May I ask in what context you came across the word?'

'Of course, Razzy.' And Twinks gave him a précis account of events at Clusters the previous night.

'So, your brother stands accused of murder?'

'Yes, but he didn't do it. Blotto wouldn't tickle a tadpole. The thought of him coffinating someone . . . except of course on behalf of His Majesty the King . . . or if he was being attacked by stenchers in foreign parts . . . well, it's about as likely as seeing a nun at a regimental dinner.'

'Hmm. Well, leave it with me, Twinks my dear. Oh, one thing . . .'

'What is it? Uncage the ferrets.'

'Are you expecting the word "Aristotours" to be connected with legitimate or criminal activities?'

'Good questionette, Razzy.' She paused before saying judiciously, 'I think it's likely to be a legitimate enterprise acting as a front for something as niffy as a six-month Stilton.'

'Thank you.' Professor Erasmus Holofernes had great faith in Twinks's judgement in all matters. 'I will get back to you as soon as possible. And if that happens to be during the night . . . ?'

'Better wait till daylight, Razzy. Say, after nine. Don't want to put a jumping cracker under the whole of Tawcester Towers.'

'Very well. Expect a call from me at nine o'clock sharp in the morning.'

'Splendissimo!' murmured Twinks.

She was still wakeful when she returned to her boudoir, so she thought a little light research of her own might be in order. Her bookshelves boasted a copy of Burke's Peerage, along with other works of genealogy, and she checked through them for the history of the Viscounts Washbourne. So many titles had been purchased recently, she wondered whether the murder victim was another *parvenu*. Like that oikish sponge-worm Sir Percy Sparkes, Bart, next to whom she'd been seated at the Clusters dinner in what felt like another century.

No, the Washbournes did turn out to have some breeding. Not on the scale of the Lyminsters, of course. But the title had not been bought in one of Lloyd George's rounds of personal fundraising. It dated from the time of another notorious peerage-seller, James the First of England ('and Sixth of Scotland', as he was always known).

So, Viscount Washbourne was the genuine article, more or less.

But why on earth had someone wanted to murder him?

Twinks tended to take an earlier breakfast than the rest of her family. Her mother never appeared in the dining room before lunch. She had a morning tray delivered to her bedroom. Loofah and Sloggo breakfasted with their proliferation of daughters in the East Wing. And Blotto rarely showed up before nine thirty to embark on the gargantuan feast with which he kept himself going for the day ahead ... at least until lunchtime.

That morning was a dull one for September, promising an unsettled winter ahead. The rain had continued all night and showed not the slightest intention of stopping.

Twinks was toying with a devilled kidney, when Grimshaw the butler approached and announced deferentially that there was a telephone call for her. As she walked to the door, she checked the large clock over the fireplace. Nine o'clock, bong on the nose.

'Hello, Razzy.'

'My dear Twinks, I hope I am not disturbing your slumbers.'

'No, up and into the devilled kidney nosebags.'

'Then I hope I am not disturbing your breakfast.'

'Not at all. Still plenty of chops in the chafing dishes. So, Razzy, have you come up with the silverware?'

'Of course I have.' He sounded a little peeved that she might have doubted him.

'Don't fiddle round the fir trees. Tell me all.'

'Well, my dear Twinks, your instinct was right. Aristotours is a perfectly legitimate enterprise.'

'Oh, snubbins!' she said, childishly disappointed.

'It is, as the name suggests, an organisation devoted to the rather vulgar business of tourism.'

'Then why's it shoehorned the word "Aristo" into its name-tag? Is it to give the poor thimbles who use its services ideas above their station?'

'I would imagine that is part of the intention. It is certainly true that all of the tours they run involve visits to stately homes and interaction with members of the aristocracy.'

'What's in your brainbox when you use the word "interaction", Razzy?'

'According to the Aristotours brochure, people enrolling in their tours are "guaranteed to meet and mix with genuine members of the aristocracy".'

'Great whiffling water rats!' To use such language, Twinks was clearly shocked. 'Which would explain that gluepot of a dinner at Clusters.'

'It would indeed, my dear Twinks. My researches reveal that that event was definitely organised by Aristotours. It was advertised in an old brochure.'

'"Advertised"?' She was appalled. 'I never in my bornies expected to hear that word used in the same sentence as "aristocrat".'

'I'm afraid "aristocrat" is a word of widening definition these days.'

'You're bong on the nose there, Razzy. We can thank Lloyd George for that. And who is the slugbucket behind this horracious Aristotours enterprise?'

'That's where the situation become interesting, my dear Twinks. There is a board of directors, most of whose names mean nothing to me and who all seem to be businessmen of no particular distinction. But there is one with a title.'

'Oh?'

'Baron Chipping Norton.'

'I met the stencher at Clusters.'

'So you told me. It would seem that he is on the board as an adviser to the company on the behaviour of aristocrats.'

'Chipping Norton's not an aristocrat! Or he only has been for the fluttering of a butterfly's eyelash.' Twinks sounded disappointed and disconsolate as she asked, 'Is that all you've got, Razzy?'

It seemed unlikely. Professor Erasmus Holofernes's researches were usually more productive. She waited hopefully until he announced, 'There is more. Something I cannot prove at this point, but something of which I have a strong suspicion.'

'Come on, Razzy. Uncage the ferrets.'

'When we spoke last night, my dear Twinks, you expressed the view that Aristotours might be a respectable, legitimate front for a business whose activities were considerably less legitimate.'

'You're the right side of right there, Razzy.'

'Well, as I say, I cannot currently confirm the connection – more research will be required for that, and I already have it in hand – but I have a strong instinct that there is a link between Aristotours and . . .' there was in his voice a note of terror that Twinks had not heard before '. . . the Crooked Hand.'

'"The Crooked Hand"?' she echoed. 'And what are they when they've got their spats on?' This was an unusual response from Twinks. Normally, like the Professor, she knew everything about everything. Indeed, she would have known more about the Crooked Hand had her brother mentioned the reference to it made by Viscount Washbourne at Clusters. Though, of course, at the time Blotto had thought his dinner companion was talking about people cheating at bridge.

'The Crooked Hand,' whispered Professor Erasmus Holofernes, still sounding shaken, but also awestruck, 'is a conspiracy of international Anarchists, whose avowed intention is to take over all the institutions of the world.'

'Larksissimo!' murmured Twinks. 'I've always liked a challenge.'

71

10

Questions, Questions . . .

'Anarchist?' Blotto echoed. His sister had returned to the dining room after her phone call and found him raiding the chafing dishes for his usual lavish rations of bacon, eggs, sausages, kedgeree, kippers, and devilled kidneys. There was no one else present, so they could talk about private matters.

'You do know what I mean by "Anarchist", don't you?'

'Yes, I do, by Denzil!' There was a silence. 'The question is: who?'

'I beg your parsnips?'

'Who did Anna kiss? And did the poor thimble mind when she kissed him?'

'No, sorry, we're not on the same page, Blotters. Basically, Anarchists are slugbuckets who want to reverse the established order.'

'What, you mean they want to start with Z rather than A?'

'Metaphorically.'

'No, I haven't.'

'Haven't what?'

'Met a Forickly. In fact, not to shuffle round the shrubbery, I have to admit that I don't know what a Forickly is.'

'Don't don your worry-boots, Blotters.' Twinks knew there were times with her brother when explanation was not worth the effort. 'All you need to know is that Anarchists are lumps of toadspawn. Four-faced filchers. They don't even know the rules of cricket, let alone play by them.'

'The fugworms!' said Blotto, with feeling. 'Then they must be stopped.'

'Give that pony a rosette!' said Twinks. 'And if they have got their fingers in this Aristotours gluepot, I'm relying on you to get the gin-gen.'

This was odd. It was unusual for Twinks to rely on her brother to do anything that didn't involve muscle power or being noble and brave. 'How am I going to get the gin-gen?'

'As ever, you get the gin-gen from the boddos who have the gin-gen, the customary sources of information. Has it trickled out through the colander of your brain where you're going this morning?'

'No,' replied Blotto, with his customary honesty.

'This morning, my dear bro, you are pongling along to Tawsworthy police station to answer further questions about the death of Viscount Washbourne. According to your bail conditions.'

'Ah, yes, by Denzil! That had rather slipped through the strainer.'

'And, while you are there, you're going to truffle out as much as you can about the background to the murder.' A silence. 'Aren't you?'

'Tickey-tockey!' said her brother enthusiastically.

Meanwhile, as per arrangement, Rodney Perkins continued his work on the replacement of the Tawcester Towers boiler. By now, every morning there arrived a surprising number of vans, containing a surprising number of workmen. It might have been wondered whether, though the plumber himself seemed ready to work for extensively delayed payment (or possibly none at all), his staff would be so ready to defer their remuneration? But none of the Lyminster family would have thought to ask questions like that. Except for Twinks, and her mind was on other things. Chiefly Anarchists.

Rodney Perkins's workforce brought a considerable amount of equipment into Tawcester Towers, though again none of the Lyminsters could have said what any of it was for. It did not belong to the aristocracy to know about such things. If they had thought to question why the workmen needed to go into so many of Tawcester Towers' many rooms, they might have considered it was something to do with checking the radiators. But none of them thought like that either. To the Lyminsters, members of the servant classes were genuinely invisible.

Blotto hadn't just forgotten that he was due to be at Tawsworthy police station on the Monday morning. It had also completely slipped his mind that he'd been charged with murder. So, having driven into town through the relentless rain and been sat down in the station office, he was slightly surprised when his police reception committee raised the matter.

As well as Chief Inspector Trumbull and Sergeant Knatchbull, there was a third person there to question him. Sir Albert Anstruther, Chief Constable of Tawcestershire. Although a relatively common occurrence due to the concentration of stately homes in the county, a murder was always worthy of his attention.

His presence ensured that Trumbull and Knatchbull would be absolutely silent, unless they were asked to contribute to the discourse. Both officers, as ever knowing their place, just sat there, faces fixed in their customary expressions of bafflement.

Sir Albert was, of course, known to the accused. The Chief Constable had frequently been entertained at Tawcester Towers, where he was treated with that mixture of pity and condescension which the Lyminsters visited on all members of the aristocracy lower than they were in the hierarchy. Blotto saw no reason to behave differently in his new role as someone accused of murder.

Sir Albert Anstruther had, as ever, the look of someone at the end of a high diving board who has just thought better of diving but doesn't want to lose face by going back down the ladder.

'Well,' he said, with an attempt at breeziness, 'you seem to have got yourself into something of a spot, Lord Devereux.'

'Oh, please call me "Blotto".'

'I'm not sure that's quite appropriate in the circumstances.'

'But you always call me "Blotto" with the Mater back at T.T.'

'That's hardly the point. I don't think I should call you "Blotto" in the presence of . . .' He gestured towards Trumbull and Knatchbull. 'You wouldn't want them to call you "Blotto", would you?'

'For the love of strawberries, no! That'd be way beyond the barbed wire.'

'So, perhaps, in these circumstances, it would be better if I were not to call you "Blotto".'

The accused shrugged. 'No skin off my rice pudding, Bertie.'

The Chief Constable winced. 'I think also, by the same token, it might be better if you were not to call me "Bertie".'

'Why not, in the name of snitchrags?'

'Well, erm . . . It just doesn't seem right.'

'What should I call you then?'

'Chief Constable?'

75

Blotto shrugged again. 'No icing off my birthday cake,' he said, 'Chief Constable.'

'Thank you.' Sir Albert Anstruther cleared his throat. 'Now, as you know, Lord Devereux, this is a murder inquiry. Viscount Washbourne was definitely killed by a knife stabbed into his back and, at the moment, there is a lot of evidence that you were the one who put it there.'

'Don't talk such meringue. You know I didn't do it, Bertie.'

'And how do I know that?'

'Because ... Do I have to spell it out in block capitals? ... Like you, old boy, I went to Eton.'

'More to the point, Lord Devereux,' the Chief Constable said, as if he were making a pronouncement of great significance, 'the murder victim also went to Eton, where he was your exact contemporary. And yet you claimed never to have met him.'

'Bertie, how many times do I have to put on the same cylinder? The poor greengage didn't play cricket. Hence, I never clapped my peepers on him.'

'But he had a title. Surely, back at the old school, you would have been aware of the presence of a Viscount Washbourne?'

This did give Blotto pause. Though legitimately ignoring sons of accountants and solicitors who had been shoe-horned into Eton, he had at least tended to know the names of his titled muffin-toasters. For a moment he looked, if not nonplussed, far from nonminussed.

Rescue came from an unexpected source. The rumble of Chief Inspector Trumbull's voice was heard as he said, 'I think I can explain that, Chief Constable. I have some information on the subject.'

Bertie Anstruther looked almost as crabwhacked as Blotto. It was so rare for members of the Tawcestershire Constabulary to have any information. Normally, they knew their place and just looked baffled. And for Trumbull to have information about Old Etonians . . . He awaited the Inspector's pronouncement with interest.

'It seems, Chief Constable . . .' Trumbull began, as ever at his own pace, 'that Viscount Washbourne only inherited the title on the death of a distant cousin last year. At school he was known as "Nigel Wickerstaff".'

'"Wickerstaff",' said Blotto.

'I'm sorry, milord?'

'You have to understand, Trumbull, no one had a first name at Eton. So, the poor pineapple who became Viscount Washbourne would just have been known as "Wickerstaff".'

'Very good, milord.'

'Anyway . . .' Blotto turned to the Chief Constable. 'We went through all this rombooley at Clusters. Wickerstaff didn't play cricket when he was at the old Eton crammers, so of course I didn't know the poor thimble.'

'I'm not sure I believe you,' said Sir Albert Anstruther.

'Rein in the roans, Bertie. Let's go another way round the shrubbery. What did this Wickerstaff boddo's father do?'

'I've no idea.'

'Do you know, Trumbull?'

'The Viscount Washbourne's father was a solicitor.'

'There you are then.' Blotto spread his hands wide, as he looked directly at the Chief Constable. 'Of course I didn't know the oikish sponge-worm.'

'Hm.' Anstruther looked uncomfortable. 'Then we come on to the matter of the papers that Viscount Washbourne passed on to you at the dinner on Saturday night . . .'

'Tickey-tockey.'

'Why did he give them to you?'

'That's not a tough cashew to crack. I was sitting next to him. If you'd been sitting next to him, Bertie, he'd have passed the flipmadoodle to you.'

The Chief Constable looked dubious. 'And did you read the documents he gave you?'

'Great Wilberforce, no!'

'Why not?'

'They were of no spoffing interest to me!'

'Why not?'

'Oh, for the love of strawberries, Bertie! Stop playing "Round and round the garden"!'

'Are you saying, Lord Devereux, that you didn't look at the documents at all?'

'I read one word.'

'Ahah!' said the Chief Constable, as if he'd just cracked the alibi of a Chicago gang-leader. 'And what was the word?'

'Aristotours,' replied Blotto.

'And does that mean anything to you?'

'It means as much as a frying pan does to a flapper.'

That prompted another 'Hm' from Sir Albert. Followed by, 'Then we must return to the matter of the knife found in the back of the Viscount Washbourne, the weapon that actually killed him.'

'What about it?'

'It did have your name on it.'

'Yes.' Blotto sighed. 'Listen, Bertie, I know when it comes to the brainbox department, I'm a bit of an empty revolver.' He was displaying admirable self-knowledge. 'But even I ... even the most stupid numbnoddy in the world, someone who had spent all of his schooldays standing in the corner with a dunce's cap on ... would not coffinate someone using a knife that has his own name on it.'

'Well, I'm not so sure that—'

'If the poor droplet had had a knife with his own name on it sticking out of his back, would you think you were turning your trufflers on a case of suicide?'

'No,' replied the Chief Constable, who fancied himself as something of a detective. 'I would think that you had taken the knife from the place setting next to yours at dinner, in order to disguise your identity.'

'So, the coffinator's still wearing my name-tag, is he?'

'I'm afraid, until we find another candidate for the role, yes, he is. At the moment, Lord Devereux, you are the prime suspect. And I have to tell you that the prospects for that situation changing . . . are not looking very good.'

11

Yet More Questions

It was rather tiresome, thought Blotto, though not the first time he had found himself in the same position. The only way to get him off the meat hook was to identify the real coffinator. As soon as he returned to Tawcester Towers, he would get Twinks to focus her mighty intellect on the problem.

Thinking of Twinks reminded him that his sister had instructed him that morning to truffle out as much as he could about the background to the murder. 'So, Bertie,' he said, 'anything you can tell me about the background to the murder?'

'I'm sure I don't know any more than you do.'

'Sorry? Not on the same page?'

'Well,' the Chief Constable explained reasonably, 'if, as seems to be the case, Lord Devereux, you committed the murder, then you will know more about the background to the case than anyone else.'

'Good ticket,' said Blotto. 'I read your semaphore. So, you reckon you've got enough gubbins on me to make an arrest?'

'You already have been arrested, Lord Devereux. You were arrested on Saturday evening.'

'Oh yes, so I was. Sorry, slipped through the strainer.'

'You're currently on bail, but that doesn't mean the charge of murder has gone away.'

'No, no. Fair biddles.' There was a silence before Blotto added generously, 'And I can see absolutely why you've got the wrong end of the sink plunger. Me discovered at the scene of the crime, my knife in the victim's back, his blood on my hands . . . yes, it's an easy mistake to make.'

'Thank you,' said the Chief Constable with an edge of irony.

'What you haven't got, Bertie . . . which puts a bit of a burst in your blimp . . . is a motive. Why would I want to coffinate some poor pineapple I'd never seen before?'

'I'm sure we will find the reason, Lord Devereux,' said Sir Albert implacably, 'before your case comes to court.'

'Well . . .' Blotto smiled pleasantly. 'Wish you the fruitiest, but I think, without a motive, you'll be stuck up a chimney with the sweep's brush behind you.'

'I will take that risk.'

At that moment, there was a loud knocking at the police station door. Sergeant Knatchbull went to see who it was and found himself confronted with a drenched messenger boy carrying a package wrapped in oilskin. 'Delivery, sir,' he said, holding it forward.

Knatchbull knew the dangers currently being offered to the authorities by Anarchists, usually in the form of bombs, so he asked, suspiciously, 'Who's it from?'

'Baron Chipping Norton.'

'Oh, that's all right then.' The Sergeant took the parcel. He reckoned toffs could always be trusted . . . unless, of course, they were accused of murder. 'Do you know what's in it?'

'Yes,' the messenger boy replied. 'It's the motive which explains why Lord Devereux Lyminster killed Viscount Washbourne.'

'Thank you very much,' said Sergeant Knatchbull and closed the door, shutting out the pouring rain.

The interchange had been heard from the office, so the Sergeant did not have to spell out what he had with him. 'Maybe you should look at this, Chief Constable,' he said, humbly handing over the package.

'I think I definitely should.' Sir Albert Anstruther fastidiously refrained from touching it. 'After you've removed the damp packaging.'

As he followed instructions and started to unwrap the oilskin, Sergeant Knatchbull observed that it was 'still raining cats and dogs out there'.

'Yes, I had the Lag's roof up on the way over,' Blotto agreed. He listened for a moment. 'Is there a spoffing leak somewhere in here? I thought I heard dripping.'

'No,' said Chief Inspector Trumbull, offended by any criticism of his domain. 'Tawsworthy police station is absolutely watertight.' Then he added, with surprising vindictiveness, 'Like the case against you will soon be, milord.'

Blotto thought that was a bit beyond the barbed wire but he made no comment. He watched as Sergeant Knatchbull removed the protective cover. On it was printed the single word: 'SCOTCH'. He registered that the oilskin must have been used before to wrap a bottle of whisky.

The Chief Constable, having first donned a pair of rubber gloves, extricated a document from the envelope Knatchbull had handed to him, and read it. He turned a pitying eye on Blotto. 'I'm afraid, Lord Devereux, what I have here rather puts the seal on the deal.'

'Oh? What in the name of ginger is it?'

'Read.' Sir Albert thrust the paper towards him. 'But don't touch.' Blotto looked at him for an explanation. 'Fingerprints.'

The document was a handwritten letter, headed 'Eton College'. Although it was dated some fifteen years previously, the notepaper looked crisp and new.

Blotto read, 'Dear Lyminster, I don't know much about cricket, but I do know it has rules, which I think are called "laws". And obedience to those laws is what makes a gentleman and an Etonian. Now, all the boddoes in the school think you are a fine example of those principles.

'I, however, know differently. I don't normally go to the Cricket Pavilion, since the game bores me to tears. It seems to go on for ever, but my opinion is not what counts here. The important thing is that during last week's Eton and Harrow match, I was delegated to go to the Cricket Pavilion to deliver a message to Mr Waynestride, one of the beaks whom you know well. It was suggested I should go there at teatime, when Mr Waynestride would not be on the pitch, to deliver the message. While looking for him, I ended up in the home team's dressing room.

'The only person there was you, Lyminster. Everyone else was scoffing their tea. You did not see me, but I witnessed what you were doing. You were holding the match ball in one hand. In the other you had a nail file, which you were scraping against the leather surface of the ball.'

Blotto could not suppress the response that burst out of him. 'The little stencher! He's accusing me of ball-tampering!'

None of the other three said anything as he read on, 'I know enough about cricket to know that what you were doing was against the laws.

'I am not planning to do anything at the moment, Lyminster, but never forget that I have this knowledge which could put a kibosh on your reputation as a clean-cut, honourable Englishman. When the moment is right, I may start telling people about what I saw in the Cricket Pavilion. So, watch your step, Lyminster.

'Yours sincerely,

'Wickerstaff.'

Blotto looked with bewilderment at the three representatives of the Police Force. 'Where did this piece of globbins come from?' he asked.

'The Earl of Woking rang me about it this morning,'

replied the Chief Constable. 'It was found by one of the maidservants who was tidying your room.'

'Which room?' asked Blotto.

'The room which you were allocated for your stay at Clusters.'

'Well, that proves this whole thing's a lump of lead-penny shiffling. I didn't have a spoffing room at Clusters! My sister and I just went for the Saturday night dinner. We didn't book in for the whole weekend rombooley.'

'Let's not worry about where the letter was found,' said the Chief Constable sternly. 'Let's talk about its contents.'

'That won't take long. It's about as believable as four-legged clover. It's a tissue of lies, a tissue—'

'Bless you,' said Chief Inspector Trumbull.

'Lord Devereux,' demanded Sir Albert Anstruther, 'are you denying that you played cricket at Eton?'

'Toad-in-the-hole, no! But there's a difference between playing the spoffing game and playing it like a backstreet thimble-rigger!' Blotto was highly aerated. His back was broad, normally he could cope with criticism. But to accuse him of cheating at cricket! That was an offence on the scale of scratching the paintwork on his Lagonda.

'Well,' said the Chief Constable, 'I find this a very convincing document. And I'm even more convinced by the way you've reacted.'

'What do you mean?'

'Clearly, being accused of cheating at cricket touches a very raw nerve in you, Lord Devereux.'

'Well, Madeira cake crumbs, Bertie, are you surprised? Only the worst kind of slugbucket – or someone who didn't have the benefit of being brought up in this country – would contemplate cheating at cricket. A stencher who did that would face social ruin! None of the right sort of people would ever exchange any chittle-chattle with him again.'

'Exactly!' crowed the Chief Constable, as if his point had been made. 'So, if someone was threatened with being revealed as a cheat at cricket . . . then they'd certainly be prepared to commit murder to escape the accusation!'

'I agree, a boddo certainly would,' Blotto countered patiently. 'But only if he ever *had* cheated at cricket, and what you don't seem to have drilled into your brainbox yet, Bertie, is that that's something no Lyminster ever would do. There's about as much chance of that as of . . . I don't know . . . the sky falling in!'

It wasn't the sky, actually. It was the ceiling that fell in at that very moment.

The volume of rainwater that had come through the hole where Corky had removed the tiles had built up to the point where the second-floor ceiling could no longer hold it in. The dam-burst cataracted on to the landing and smashed through into the Tawsworthy police station office. Within seconds, the Chief Constable, Chief Inspector Trumbull and Sergeant Knatchbull were all soaked to the skin and covered with wet plaster.

The deluge missed Blotto, who got up, walked out to his absolutely watertight Lagonda, and drove back to Tawcester Towers.

12

A New Member of Staff

'Come on, uncage the ferrets, Blotters!' said Twinks eagerly. 'Give me the gin-gen!'

'What gin-gen?' asked her brother.

'The gin-gen you picked up at Tawsworthy police station.'

'I didn't pick up any spoffing gin-gen at Tawsworthy police station,' said Blotto.

Twinks was used to this. Her brother wasn't deliberately obtuse. Nor was he unobservant. He just sometimes needed prompting to remember details. His brain was not always efficient at distinguishing what was important from what wasn't. Or perhaps it was simply the case that, if the subject wasn't cricket or hunting, then he didn't think it was important, anyway.

So, Twinks led his recollection gently through the exact sequence of events that had unfolded at Tawsworthy police station. She was particularly interested by the sudden arrival of the motive for Blotto to kill Viscount Washbourne.

'Great spangled spiders! Someone's definitely been playing the rat's part here. There's no way that a Grade A foundation stone like you is a coffinator.'

'No-o.' Blotto sounded strangely uncertain. 'But the filchers had done their homework.'

'Sorry? Not on the same page?'

'Well, though I pride myself that I never *would* coffinate anyone, except on behalf of His Majesty or to save a woman's honour or in self-defence, the one thing that might push me over the edge of the razor blade is an accusation of ball-tampering.'

'But you're no more likely to tamper with a ball than you are to coffinate someone.'

'You're bong on the nose there, Twinks.'

'But you're right. Those lumps of toadspawn had done their homework.' Twinks focused her azure eyes on the lighter blue of her brother's. 'Now come on, tune up the brainbox. Was there anything else you remember about the letter?'

'The one they showed me, the one that came from Viscount Washbourne? From Wickerstaff, as the thimble was known back then?'

'That one, yes. Except, of course, it didn't come from him. Some stencher cobbled it up.'

'Yes, they did, by Denzil!'

'Anything else you remember about the letter?' Blotto shook his head glumly. 'Or about the envelope?' Another shake. 'Or the oilskin it was wrapped in?'

Blotto stopped his head in mid-shake and a wide beam irradiated his features. 'Ah, something has blipped the old brain cells there, yes.'

'Splendissimo!' murmured Twinks. 'What?'

'I think the oilskin had previously been used to wrap up some whisky.'

'What tickled that thoughtette?'

'A word which was printed on the oilskin.'

'What was it?'

'"Scotch",' said Blotto dramatically.

'Now that could be particularly important,' said Twinks. She had an instinct for such things.

'Why? In what way?'

'I'm not sure yet, but I'll find out. Give that pony a massive rosette. You really are the lark's larynx, Blotters!'

'Oh, Twinks,' he said, 'don't talk such meringue!'

But, secretly, he was pleased by what she'd said.

It continued to rain all that Monday. And all that Monday, Rodney Perkins and his fellow artisans continued doing whatever it was they had been doing for weeks all over Tawcester Towers.

Round teatime, Blotto and Twinks received a summons which was strange in two ways. First, they were summoned to the Blue Morning Room, which (for obvious reasons of nomenclature) was rarely used in the afternoon. And second, the call came from Loofah, whereas everyone knew that the Blue Morning Room was the Dowager Duchess's domain. They both thought the Stilton was a bit iffy.

And, when they got there, it was clear, as ever, who was in charge. Their mother was enthroned in her customary chair and the current Duke of Tawcester stood, chinlessly apologetic as ever, to her left.

To the Dowager Duchess's right, dressed discreetly in a black suit, stood a man neither of them recognised.

And at the back of the room, having just closed the door behind Blotto and Twinks, stood Grimshaw, the Tawcester Towers butler. He wore the inscrutable expression of all butlers, for whom scrutability is a serious dereliction of duty.

The two younger Lyminsters were allowed to sit and, once they were in place, the Dowager Duchess nodded permission for their elder brother to begin.

'Erm . . .' said the Duke. 'Fact is, elements of change here at Tawcester Towers. Old place has been pongling on in its own sweet way for centuries.'

Good ticket, thought Blotto. That's how things always have been and exactly how they should stay for the foreseeable. But he didn't voice his views. In the Blue Morning Room, with the Dowager Duchess present, you spoke only when she deigned to speak to you.

'Erm . . . Anyway,' the Duke went hesitantly on, 'it is the view of some people . . .' A rumble of throat-clearing from his mother made him amend that statement. 'It is *my* view that we should bring Tawcester Towers into the nineteenth century.'

'*Twentieth* century,' hissed his mother.

'But, Mater,' said the Duke. 'It's currently the year nineteen twen—'

'It's still the twentieth century! Didn't they teach you anything at Eton? The century is always one on from the actual date.'

'Well, that's a rum baba,' said the Duke.

Blotto felt sympathy for his elder brother. He'd always had the same problem about counting the centuries. It didn't feel natural to him, this adding an extra hundred years rombooley. He thought it was a rum baba too.

'You were saying, Loofah . . . ?' the Dowager Duchess prompted forcefully.

'Yes.' The Duke of Tawcester gathered himself for the task ahead. 'Fact is . . . that changes are needed here at Tawcester Towers. Changes are being made by our peers . . .' (and when the Duke of Tawcester used the word, it was in its literal sense) '. . . and we mustn't be left behind in the competitive stately home business.'

Blotto wondered whether there was a competition between stately homes. To him, the concept seemed rather vulgar, the wrong sort of thing for the right sort of people to get involved in. Now that the prospect of another English Civil War seemed to be receding, competition should be kept where it belonged, on the cricket pitch.

'Which being the situation,' the Duke continued, 'the

Mater has decided ...' Another subterranean throat-clearing. 'Fact is, *I* have decided ...' He looked taken aback – *deciding things* was virgin territory to him – but quickly recovered '... that we need an extra member of staff to help bring Tawcester Towers into the ninetee ...' He quickly corrected himself '... twentieth century. So, I would like to introduce to you ...' He gestured to the man in the black suit. 'Mr Ulrich Weissfeder.'

Blotto and Twinks exchanged looks, both aware of how unusual this was. Their being introduced to Rodney Perkins the plumber had been strange, but at least the Dowager Duchess had done the honours. Her involving Loofah was unprecedented. Normally, like any mother of her breeding, she ignored him completely. When any decisions about the estate were required, she made them, without consulting anyone else (just as she had done when her late husband had been the Duke of Tawcester).

Normally, the appointment of new domestic staff was organised by Grimshaw. Twinks felt tempted to turn round to see if Loofah's announcement had dented the inscrutability of the butler's expression. But she couldn't do it while her mother's basilisk eye was on her.

The current Duke of Tawcester seemed to feel that, having spoken the new arrival's name, his obligation was fulfilled. Or he did until he heard his mother's urgent, 'Put a jumping cracker under it, Loofah!'

Reminded of his duty, he consulted a piece of paper hastily taken out of his jacket pocket and continued. 'Fact is, Mr Weissfeder is a man of extensive experience. He has spent his working life in the hotel industry in Switzerland, most recently as manager of the Grand Luxe in Geneva.

'As a result, there's not a boddo in the world better qualified than Mr Weissfeder to take over his new role as ... the Tawcester Towers Master of the Revels!'

* * *

The day porter was still on duty in St Raphael's lodge when Twinks rang later that afternoon. He put her straight through to Professor Erasmus Holofernes. After fulsome appreciation of her calling him, he asked how he could help.

'I told you about this clammy corner my bro's got himself into?'

'You did.'

'Well, the poor greengage is still in it – and possibly getting deeper in.'

'You mean the murder charge has not been dropped?'

'Bong on the nose, Razzy. The Mater put the pincers on the Chief Constable and got Blotters out on bail, but said Chief Constable still has my sib down as a coffinator.'

'How very short-sighted of him.'

'Bong on the nose again, Razzy.'

'So, my task in finding some dirt on Aristotours becomes all the more urgent?'

'Yes. Don't want to be a sopsap, but I'm v. attached to the old bro. Would hate to see him necked up to the Pearlies for a crime he didn't commit.'

'A very proper sisterly reaction. I will redouble my research efforts.'

'Splendissimo!'

'And do you have any more evidence for me?'

'Evidence of backdoor-sidling? Yes, I do, by Denzil.' And she told the Professor about the serendipitous – and extremely suspicious – delivery of Blotto's supposed motive to Tawsworthy police station. 'Clearly leadpenny,' she concluded. 'But Blotters did see this one word printed on the oilskin in which the envelope was wrapped.'

'And what was the word?'

'"Scotch".'

'"Scotch"?' Professor Erasmus Holofernes echoed. 'Now that *is* interesting.'

13

Low Life, High Life

The British aristocracy have always been good at keeping themselves separate from their inferiors. Castle walls traditionally proved effective against serfs and villeins, and in more civilised times these gave way to the green baize door. Upstairs and downstairs thus maintained their appropriate distance.

This does not mean that there was *no* contact between the two classes. Certain relationships – like the *droit de seigneur* young scions of noble families exercised over housemaids, and occasional encounters between ladies of the manor and gamekeepers – endured, but no one ever drew attention to them. Some aristocrats, however, did find it useful to have, if not a spy in the domestic camp, at least someone of the lower orders willing to keep them informed about what was going on down there. In Blotto's case, that person was Corky Froggett.

It was the young master's habit, of a morning, after he had downed his gargantuan cooked breakfast, to go to the stables to commune with his hunter Mephistopheles. Once horse and man had put the world to rights, man would frequently go to visit his Lagonda, another of the three loves in his life (the third, in case you'd forgotten, being his cricket bat).

There he would inevitably encounter the chauffeur, who had just completed the polishing of the bodywork to an unimpeachable shine. Master and servant might then continue their endless duologue about the engineering brilliance of the car. Or, if there was something Blotto wanted to know about – or Twinks had told him to find out about – events below stairs, Corky would be requested to come up with the dirt.

The chauffeur had an excellent information network among the Tawcester Towers staff, particularly the cooks and housemaids. He was close (extremely close, in some cases) to them.

The morning after Mr Weissfeder's appointment, both Blotto and Twinks were eager to find out the reverberations of the event beyond the green baize door, and Corky Froggett was more than ready to satisfy their curiosity.

'Well, you're not going to bring in someone over Grimshaw's head and find him very happy about it, are you? And this Weissflapper or whatever his name is, certainly isn't one for the tactful approach. He doesn't give a monkey's about old Grimshaw's nose being out of joint. Starts ordering him around, as if he's not the Tawcester Towers butler but some teenage boot boy on his first day at the place.

'And then, just when you'd have thought things couldn't get worse, he started having a go at Harvey.'

At this, Blotto and Twinks inhaled synchronised breaths. Harvey was one of the housemaids, older than the others, with a tendency to wear shorter skirts and lower-cut blouses than they did. It was well known in Tawcester Towers that a certain *tendresse* existed between Grimshaw and Harvey. The Dowager Duchess kept urging him to make an honest woman of her, but the butler continued in the view that that would be too difficult a task. The rest of the staff, however, knew that any criticism of Harvey would land them very firmly in Grimshaw's black books.

'Anyway, our new Master of the Revels started having a go at the way Harvey dresses. He said this was an English stately home, not the Bois de Boulogne.'

'Sorry? Not on the same page?' said Blotto.

'It is an area of Paris, milord, frequented by ladies of the night.'

'Oh? Who frequents it in the daytime?'

Corky Froggett looked hopefully towards Twinks, who shook her head slightly, indicating he should not stop to explain.

'Anyway, milord, our new Master of the Revels said that Harvey looked like a sloven and a slut and a slag and a . . . what's another word beginning with S-L?'

'Sledge?' suggested Blotto, pleased that the question was so easy.

'Slattern?' proposed Twinks.

'That's it, milady – slattern! Well, you can imagine – Grimshaw wasn't best pleased by that. Nor was Harvey, now I come to think of it. And then Weissfumbler goes into this rant, in his mimsy-pimsy Swiss accent – that all of the Tawcester Towers uniforms look pretty scruffy and how we was all going to have to pull our socks up if we was going to work in any organisation he was running.'

'I bet that put lumps in everyone's custard,' said Twinks.

'It certainly did, milady. But Weissflogger wasn't finished with that. Then he turned on the kitchen staff.'

'Toad-in-the-hole!' said Blotto.

'Lordie in a chicken coop!' said Twinks.

They both knew how particularly sensitive that department was. The nursery food the Tawcester Towers kitchens served up for every meal was devoid of imagination. And indeed of variety. And taste, come to that. But the above stairs residents dutifully chewed their way through it without complaint. It was what they had eaten in school and what the gentlemen continued to eat in their London clubs. People who made a fuss about any aspect of food other than its volume were nitpicking, effete . . . or French.

The Roast Beef of Old England, the Lyminsters knew, could stand up to as much mustard as the individual wished to slather it with, but should never be sullied by such decadent novelties as herbs, garnishes or, worst of all, sauces.

The newly arrived Master of the Revels had clearly set himself on a collision course with the kitchens. And the detail Corky Froggett then provided only made the matter worse.

'I heard this from one of the kitchen maids . . .' He cleared his throat. They were both too tactful to ask how close he was to the kitchen maid. 'Mr Weissfiddler issued a series of instructions. He said that at all meals more vegetables should be served.'

'Well, I'll be battered like a pudding!' said Blotto.

'And that those vegetables should be boiled for less than an hour!'

'Great spangled spiders!' said Twinks.

'Herbs should be introduced to all meals!'

'Toppling toadstools!' said Blotto.

'Steak should not be served nearly black. It should be served pink!'

'Great galumphing goatherds!' said Twinks.

'And a new chef should be appointed, whose sole job will be the creation of sauces!'

'You're jiggling my kneecap!' said Twinks.

'No, it's God's truth,' said Corky Froggett.

Blotto and Twinks looked at each other. Tawcester Towers had not faced a threat on this scale since the Wars of the Roses.

Loofah was surprised to encounter his younger siblings in his part of the house. Following the aristocratic tradition of seeing as little of family members as possible, Blotto and Twinks rarely ventured into the East Wing. It was too full of excess nieces for their taste.

Loofah's study, to which they were directed, was completely bare. There were no books on the bookshelves. The Duke of Tawcester didn't read and, since hardly anyone else ever came into the room, there was no one to impress by the range of his reading matter. Guests who needed impressing could be taken to Tawcester Towers' magnificent library and gaze at the leather spines of unopened books (unaware of the even more impressive literary resources of Twinks's boudoir).

The surface of the Duke's desk was empty too, another indicator of the fullness of his life. There was no telephone. The Duke, like everyone else, had to go to the hall if he needed to make a call. But he never did.

In fact, his life was as empty as his desk. Since his mother took all decisions relating to the estate, apart from a dutiful amount of chasing foxes and massacring birds and an annual visit to London for the House of Lords Christmas lunch, the Duke of Tawcester didn't do anything.

Except, of course, for the rigorous pursuit of his one enduring obligation, the getting of a male heir to inherit the dukedom. His dogged efforts in that cause explained both the pallor of his wife Sloggo and the large number of anaemic daughters who infested the East Wing.

Though they hadn't seen much of each other while growing up at Tawcester Towers, Loofah and Blotto had been at Eton together, so it might be thought that they would have some points of contact. But that was not the case. Neither had excelled academically and, though the older brother had played cricket, he had shown no signs of the younger's exceptional talent. The two had seen little of each other at school.

And, though they had been forced together at various family occasions over the years, Loofah hardly knew Twinks at all. And he was certainly unaware of her exceptional intellect. His experience of Sloggo and his daughters, together with his own lack of one, had not suggested to him that women had intellects. Or even articulacy.

So, he was somewhat taken aback, in his study that afternoon, when Twinks demanded, 'Loofah, what in the name of strawberries is going on?'

'Going on where?' he asked cautiously.

'Here at Tawcester spoffing Towers.'

The Duke looked out of the window before replying, 'Erm . . . Well, the same sort of things as usually go on here this time of year.'

'No, Loofah, you're not on the same page. I meant, what's going on with this Master of the Revels rombooley?'

'Well . . .' said the Duke. Then another tentative 'Erm . . . Fact is, Twinks, that Tawcester Towers . . . erm . . . does now have . . . erm . . . a Master of the Revels.'

'I know that, you pot-brained pineapple!' came the sharp response.

Loofah had never heard his sister talk to him like that before. He rather liked it. It reminded him of how his mother had always treated him.

'The questionette we need to ask,' Twinks went on, 'is *why* Tawcester Towers has a Master of the Revels.'

'Erm . . . Well, because that's what the Mater said we were going to have.'

'Then why, rather than the Mater herself doing it, did you tell us about the appointment?'

'Ah, well . . . that was for Mr Weissfeder's benefit. The Mater thought he should get the impression that, within a ducal household, the Duke should be the one in charge.'

'Even though, at Tawcester Towers,' suggested Blotto, 'that's a load of globbins.'

'Exactly.' The Duke thought the idea of his being in charge so funny that he roared with laughter. His brother joined in.

Twinks tried to get them back to the matter in hand. 'So, Loofah, did you have anything to do with the appointment of Mr Ulrich Weissfeder?'

The Duke looked at her, amazed that she should ask such a question. 'Of course not. The Mater did all that stuff.'

'So, do you know where she found him?'

'No. Do they have shops for Masters of the Revels?' Loofah's hold on the real world had always been tenuous.

Twinks didn't bother answering that. 'It just seems a bit of a rum baba, the Mater suddenly finding a plumber and a Master of the Revels within weeks of each other. Doesn't pluck the right string with me. Haven't clapped your peepers on any suspicious guests round Tawcester Towers recently, have you, Loofah?'

'"Suspicious guests"?'

Blotto felt called upon to explain. 'Boddoes pongling around the place who aren't usually pongling about the place.'

'Erm, I don't think so,' said the Duke.

Twinks persisted, 'Anyone rat-tatting on the Mater's door who doesn't usually come rat-tatting on the Mater's door?'

'Erm . . . No.' Her older brother looked perplexed (this was actually his permanent expression). 'Erm . . . Well. Only Baron Chipping Norton.'

14

Blotto Takes Things into His Own Hands

'It's spoffing tiresome,' Blotto complained. 'Just because a boddo's been accused of murder, the police won't leave a boddo alone.'

He and Twinks had returned from the East Wing to a message from Grimshaw asking him to ring the Chief Constable. And on the telephone Bertie Anstruther had had the gall to suggest that further questioning about the death of Viscount Washbourne was required. No other lead having led anywhere, Blotto remained the prime suspect for the crime.

Whatever – the accused asked himself – had happened to the sacred principle of the old boy network? He and Bertie hadn't actually toasted the same muffins in the same year but they'd both been at Eton. Surely that ought to count for something?

They were back in Twinks's boudoir. She was absorbed, consulting her various books of genealogy and peerage to find out more about Baron Chipping Norton, but making little headway. Clearly, he was another who had only recently bought his title, when Lloyd George was flogging them like a Billingsgate fishmonger, and it had yet to be catalogued. She was thinking she might need to make another call to Professor Erasmus Holofernes.

Not getting any response from his sister, Blotto went on, 'It seems like Baron Chipping Norton is the four-faced filcher behind all this sneakery, doesn't it?' Still nothing from Twinks. 'I mean, he was at Clusters when Viscount Washbourne was coffinated.' Silence. 'It was a messenger from him who brought that leadpenny letter from Wickerstaff to Tawsworthy police station.' Enduring silence. 'And now, according to Loofah, he's the one who's been finding plumbers and other pondlife for the Mater. So, it's as clear as the *consommé* at Claridge's that the Chief Slugbucket is none other than . . . Baron Chipping Norton!'

'We don't have any proof at the moment,' said Twinks distractedly. 'We're a long way off fingering the felon. We don't want to start counting our blue tits before they're born. We need to snail it a bit for the moment.'

'Fair biddles,' said Blotto with a note of bitterness. 'Or it would be fair biddles if Bertie Anstruther agreed to snail it a bit on his investigation too. Do you think that's likely, though? There's a serious poss that, while we're snailing it, I could end up being found guilty of murder!'

'Puddledash, Blotters! We know you're not the coffinator and we'll soon prove it!'

'How, in the name of ginger?'

'Leave it with me,' said Twinks, still abstracted. 'I'll focus my feelers on it when I've got some more gin-gen on Baron Chipping Norton.'

'Good ticket,' said Blotto, hoping his sister was aware of the sarcasm that he put into the words. He could hurt when he needed to.

Blotto rarely got angry with Twinks. His normal attitude to her was fixed somewhere between worship and adoration. But her offhand manner that afternoon made him close the boudoir door behind him with more than usual force.

It also made him question whether he had to wait till she was ready to pursue their investigations. Or whether he might make more headway on his own . . . ?

Corky Froggett was just completing the Lagonda's second daily cleaning, to remove any specks of dust which might have had the temerity to settle on the blue bodywork since its morning polish. He looked up as the young master approached.

'Good afternoon, milord. Do you wish to take her out for a spin?'

'No, thanks, Corky. I've got bigger fish in the frying pan than knocking vicars off bicycles.'

'Very good, milord.'

'And I need some gin-gen from you. Need to dibble about in your brains, Corky.'

'You're welcome to anything you may find there, milord.'

'Could you roll the old mind back to the evening of that dinner at Clusters?'

Corky Froggett was far too tactful to mention that that was the evening when the young master had been accused of murder. He just said, 'Certainly, milord.'

'Well, while the sis and I were busy with the chittle-chattle and the nosebags above stairs, you were consorting with the domestics below stairs?'

'Yes, milord.' The chauffeur didn't speak of the dis-appointment he had felt that evening about the Clusters kitchen maid, with whom he had hoped to pick up where he had left off. She turned out to have lost interest in the idea of 'the older man' and embarked on a romance with the youngest and spottiest of the boot boys.

'And I dare say, Corky, that at such times there's a certain amount of whiffle-waffle exchanged about your various employers?'

101

Corky was quick to counter any imputation of inappropriate behaviour. 'I can assure you, milord, that I have never revealed any secrets about you ... or other members of the Lyminster family.'

'Don't don your worry-boots about that. I know you're a Grade A foundation stone, Corky. You wouldn't dollop the dirt on us under torture.'

'That is true, milord. Rack, thumbscrews, Iron Maiden, let them try their worst. I would regard it as an honour to give up my life with maximum pain in your service.' A mistiness came into the chauffeur's eyes as he visualised his most precious dream.

'You're a good greengage, Corky,' said Blotto. 'Anyway, the gin-gen I'm after concerns a lump of toadspawn called Baron Chipping Norton. I wonder if, by any chance, that evening at Clusters, you exchanged any whiffle-waffle with members of his retinue?'

'I did indeed, milord. I spent some time in conversation with Baron Chipping Norton's valet. A young person of unprepossessing manners and appearance, it has to be said.'

'So, did you find out where said Baron hangs up his jim-jams?'

'I did, milord. And it certainly isn't Chipping Norton!'

They both laughed at that. The idea that an aristocrat should actually live in the place featured in his title was extremely unlikely. The Duke of Norfolk lived in Arundel, nowhere near Norfolk; the Duke of Devonshire was based in Derbyshire; and so on.

When they had stopped laughing, Blotto asked, 'So where does he hitch up his horses?'

'He lives in a castle on the western borders of Tawcestershire, still within the county, milord.' Corky replied. 'Paramere Castle, it's called. He didn't inherit it, though. He bought the place.'

'The oikish sponge-worm,' said Blotto. Everyone knew

that property, like furniture, should always be inherited. Still, he shouldn't have been surprised. The kind of stencher who bought a title was capable of buying anything.

'Tell me, Corky, did this valet thimble you shared the Clusters whiffle-waffle with . . . did he say anything about what kind of a boddo Baron Chipping Norton was to work for? On the good side of the egg basket? Or a slugbucket?'

'Definitely on the slugbucket side, milord. It is often observed below stairs that persons whose family trees have no roots tend to lack the common touch. They are so insecure in their elevated positions that they take it out on their inferiors . . . who, in many cases, until relatively recently, were their equals.'

'Is that the way the carpet unrolls?' asked Blotto, who had, of course, never been in a position to doubt his own superiority over almost everyone he met.

'It is a very frequent occurrence, milord.'

'Well, I'll be snickered! Now, listen, Corky, I'm about to tell you something, but it's very important that you don't uncage the ferrets about it to anyone else.'

'As I hope we have established, milord, I am happy to keep your secrets, even in the extremities of torture.'

'You're made of pure brick-mix, Corky.'

'Thank you, milord.'

'It is my planette to go to see Baron Chipping Norton at Paramere Castle.'

'An excellent idea, milord. Will you be proposing to take the Lady Honoria with you?'

'No, this is where my plan is such a bellbuzzer. I am going to confront the Baron on my own!'

'If you think that is appropriate, milord.' This was as near as Corky Froggett dared to go in suggesting that the idea might be less than perfect. He had recollections of too many other occasions when Blotto had attempted feats of derring-do without his sister's advice. And, in some cases, even against his sister's advice. None of them had ended happily.

'What's more, Corky, I want you to keep what I've just told you fixed inside your tooth-trap with a leather strap. Twinks must not know about it!'

'Very good, milord.' This wasn't a promising sign either. Going behind Twinks's back was always the direct route to trouble. 'But I do hope, milord, you will allow me to accompany you on your mission.'

'No, Corky. This time, for once, I'm going to take things into my own hands!'

'Very good, milord.'

Though Corky couldn't pretend to himself that he thought it was very good at all.

On the extraordinarily rare occasions when Blotto needed to get up early, he had an arrangement with Grimshaw, the butler. There was no way the young master would contemplate leaving Tawcester Towers without having had his full breakfast, so, before the chafing dishes had been filled for the rest of the family, a special order (of everything) would be prepared in the kitchen and brought to the dining room for him. It would always be served by the housemaid Harvey, who owed her domestic position (and quite a lot of other positions) to her closeness to Grimshaw.

Each time Harvey put in an appearance, her skirt seemed to be shorter and her cleavage lower, but Blotto never noticed. When he had an early breakfast, his mind was always on other things. Cricket, hunting or, on this occasion, sorting everything out with Baron Chipping Norton.

The reason, incidentally, for his early breakfast on that particular day was that he wanted to avoid meeting Twinks. He knew she'd winkle out of him where he was planning to go. Then she would either dissuade him from going or insist on coming with him.

And he was determined to do this bit of the investigation on his own.

Blotto couldn't take Mephistopheles in the car, but he was still with two of his three favourite things. His cricket bat was stowed in the dickey and he was driving his Lagonda through the narrow lanes of the most beautiful country on God's earth. He murmured one of his sister's favourite expressions, 'Larksissimo', as he forced yet another vicar on a bicycle into the hedgerow.

Though Blotto had great aptitude for devising cunning strategies for the winning of cricket matches, he was not by nature a planner. He tended to think on the hoof, wait for things to happen and then sort them out. In this he differed considerably from his sister. So, his journey to Paramere Castle, seat of Baron Chipping Norton, was unclouded by thoughts of what might happen when he got there.

Paramere Castle didn't look like a castle should look. No chunks appeared to have been gouged out of it by cannon fire in the Wars of the Roses or the Civil War. If they had, they'd been mended, which went against all aristocratic principles. To add insult to lack of injury, the stonework was actually clean. So were the many windows on the castle's frontage (too many, they must have been put in to replace the defensive arrow-slits – another insult to history).

The sweep of gravel on which Blotto brought the Lagonda to a halt was far too well raked. And it was actually surrounded by flower beds with bedding plants in them! Just like the suburban garden of an accountant or a solicitor. The main doors of the castle were not scarred by the scorch-marks of ancient incendiary bombs and the blows of battering rams. They had shiny brass handles and panels of modern glass cut into them. Clearly, Baron Chipping Norton had a lot to learn about the business of being an aristocrat.

As a further demonstration of his lack of breeding, the Baron himself issued out of the ugly modern doors to greet Blotto. Didn't the boddo know, thought the new arrival, that the first contact should be with some lowly member of the servant class, like a butler? A line-up of a large number of the domestic staff was quite in order, but not just the host on his lonelio.

'Lord Devereux,' said the Baron. 'We meet again.'

'Call me Blotto. That's on my calling card.'

'Oh. My first name is Kevin.'

'Tough Gorgonzola,' said Blotto, with genuine sympathy. Then, generously, 'I'll call you "Chippers".'

'I'm not sure that—'

'Anyway, Chippers me old fruit pastille, I'm here to gab about Aristotours.'

'Yes, I had been expecting you,' said the Baron, a remark which might have raised suspicions in a sharper mind than Blotto's. 'Maybe you would like to come in and discuss the matter over a glass of sherry . . . ?'

'Tickey-tockey.'

The bad impression created by Paramere Castle's exterior was not dispelled by entering what the Baron referred to as the 'living room'. The right sort of people, amongst whom Blotto had, of course, grown up, had rooms for receiving in, dining in and withdrawing to, but generally speaking, they did their living wherever they wanted to, wherever they happened to be at any given time. They didn't have a room specifically for living in.

Nor did they shout at their butlers (or rather, they only shouted at their butlers when the said menials surprised them *in flagrante* in an inappropriate bedroom). The way Baron Chipping Norton bawled out his butler when he ordered the sherry – and when it was brought in – showed how unused he was to having servants.

Mind you, he had plenty of them, all in very new-looking livery. Half a dozen lined the hallway, and the same number stood round the walls of the living room. All were in defensive posture, as though guarding someone. This was another factor which might have tinkled the odd alarm bell in a brain sharper than Blotto's.

Apart from the servants, there was a third person present in the 'living room' as they had their sherry. Although he was indoors, the man wore a belted beige raincoat and a deeply dented fedora. The Baron introduced him as Ivor Gelatine, a private investigator.

'So, you're a boddo who investigates privately?' asked Blotto, who knew his duty when it came to making conversation.

'I find that's the best way,' came the reply, in a slow American drawl. 'Investigate publicly and people start to figure out that you're investigating.'

'Toad-in-the-hole! I hadn't thought of that,' said Blotto. 'Are you actually investigating at the moment?'

'Never stop.'

'So, what kind of four-faced filchery are you truffling into at the instant?'

Ivor Gelatine looked evenly at Baron Chipping Norton as he replied, 'I'm investigating the fraudulent activities of a company called Aristotours.'

15

Private Investigations

The Baron smiled thinly. 'I think that is slightly misleading, Mr Gelatine.' He looked at Blotto. 'What Mr Gelatine meant was that he was investigating a group of scoundrels who are trying to blacken the name of Aristotours.'

The private investigator did not take issue with this correction. Someone more sensitive to mood might have detected the crackling tension between the two men. But as ever, Blotto's barometer was set to 'Sunny', and he was prepared to think the best of all the boddoes in the world (except accountants, solicitors and Harrovians, obviously).

'What is being said,' the Baron went on, 'will soon be proved to be defamation. I know from my own involvement that Aristotours is a perfectly legitimate business.'

'Rein in the roans a moment there,' said Blotto. 'Are you telling me that Aristotours is a pie into which you have dipped the odd digit?'

'I am on the board in a non-executive capacity,' came the chilly reply.

'Oh, Tickey-tockey. Thought you meant you worked for the stenchers.' Blotto chuckled. 'Bit beyond the barbed wire for someone with a title to actually work – what?'

'I know what is appropriate to my status in society,' said the Baron.

'I'm sure you spoffing well do,' said Blotto genially. 'Important those down the lower end of the peerage don't get ideas above their station, eh?'

He felt perhaps he ought to explain this to Ivor Gelatine. Having no class system themselves, Americans were usually clueless about how such things worked. 'We have a real buzzbanger of a wheeze in the British aristocracy ... a pecking order, you might say. Dukes on top of the Christmas tree, then Marquesses, Earls, Viscounts ... and Barons down grubbing away on the floor. That's why it's called a pecking order. Each rank pecks up the spoffing crumbs from the table of their superiors. Works like a dose of Benskin's Powder, has done since the Conquest.'

'Thank you for the explanation,' said the private investigator.

'No skin off my rice pudding,' said Blotto, pleased to have brought a little enlightenment into the ignorant fog of a foreigner's mind.

He was unaware of the look of pure hatred currently focused on him by Baron Chipping Norton. He was aware, though, as he looked round the 'living room', that the assembled domestics looked more like guards with each passing minute. There seemed to be unexplained bulges in the waistbands of their uniforms. For some reason, Blotto was reminded of the time he'd spent in Chicago with a gentleman called Spagsy Chiaparelli.

'We are in a situation of extreme danger,' the Baron announced. 'The accusations against Aristotours are only a symptom of a much greater political upheaval in this country – and indeed throughout the world. There are dark forces at work.'

'Would this be the Antichrists?' asked Blotto.

'I think the word you're looking for is "Anarchists",' said the Baron.

'Oh yes. Tickey-tockey. So, are they the stenchers who're perpetrating all that rombooley you were talking about?'

'Anarchists are certainly involved,' the Baron replied, 'but what we're talking about here is a worldwide conspiracy. And I have received information that an attack on Paramere Castle by these sinister forces is planned for today!'

'Toad-in-the-hole!' said Blotto.

'So, it's particularly important that we are all armed to resist them.'

The Baron opened a drawer in a table beside his chair and took out a revolver. He reached across and put it into Blotto's hand. 'I don't like the idea of you being unarmed in such a dangerous situation.'

'Well, that's very British of you.' Blotto felt the heft of the gun in his hand. 'But I've never really fancied the fishing when it comes to slug-shifters. They don't pluck the right string with me. If there's derring-do to be derring-done, I prefer to rely on my spoffing cricket bat.'

'But surely, that wouldn't—'

'Don't worry, Baron me old trouser button. I'm ahead of the hounds here. I did bring the old cricket bat with me. Stowed in the dickey of the Lag. So, don't don your worry-boots. It's all going to be creamy éclair.'

Pleased to have reassured his host, Blotto handed the revolver back. 'And if you think the Antichrist slugbuckets will soon be on the prems, I'll go and fetch the bat, quick as a lizard's lick.'

Which is what Blotto did.

He was reaching into the Lagonda's dickey when he heard the sound of running footsteps on the gravel and turned to see Ivor Gelatine approaching. The private investigator's hard-boiled face was riven with urgency.

'Listen, buddy, you came here because you were suspicious of what was going on with Aristotours – right?'

'You're bong on the nose there.'

'Well, if it's dirt you want, I'm your man.'

'Sorry? Not on the same page?'

'Don't listen to anything that liar Baron Chipping Norton says. He was implying that I was working for him. No, it's the exact opposite. I've been investigating the dirty dealing Aristotours has been involved in and I came here this morning to confront the Baron with the evidence. But since you seem to be on the same side, I'm happy to share my findings with you.'

'That's frightfully British of you,' said Blotto. 'Particularly since you're American.'

'Don't care if it's British or Chinese,' said Gelatine. 'All I'm after is the truth.'

'Good ticket,' said Blotto.

'Look, I've compiled a dossier.'

'Have you, by Denzil?'

'You do know what a dossier is, don't you?'

'Tickey-tockey.'

'Then what is it?' asked Gelatine suspiciously. Somehow – perhaps that's what private investigators do – he seemed to have detected that Blotto wasn't the sharpest knife in the canteen.

'It's one of those poor boddoes who has to sleep in the gutter,' suggested Blotto.

'I think you'll find that's a "dosser". A "dossier" is like a file.'

'What, for cutting through the bars when you're detained at His Majesty's?'

'No, a file of paper.'

'That wouldn't be much good for cutting through bars,' said Blotto dubiously.

'Never mind,' said Ivor Gelatine with something near to exasperation. He pulled a thin green carboard folder out from his raincoat. 'This is what I mean. This contains every last detail of the criminal activities of Baron Chipping Norton's set-up.'

Blotto looked at the file. On its front was printed the single word 'Aristotours'. Just like the papers Viscount

Washbourne had thrust upon him at Clusters. He opened it and read the first sentence.

'*This dossier contains irrefutable evidence that the Aristotours company is a front for a major criminal enterprise, run from Paramere Castle by Baron Chipping Norton.*'

Blotto looked up from the page and met the stone-hard stare of the private investigator. 'So, what kind of thimble-jiggling are the squiffballs up to?'

'You name it. The legitimate business front is organising social events at stately homes.'

'Oh yes, I went to one of those wodjermaflips.'

'At those they cheat both the aristocrats whose premises they use and the middle-class suckers who buy the tickets. But that's just normal business practice.'

'Toad-in-the-hole!' said Blotto. 'You mean there are murdier things going on too?'

'Sure are. Was there a séance at the event you went to?'

'There was, by Wilberforce, yes.'

'Well, they work a lot of rackets using those. Getting bereaved people to pay through their noses for one-to-one sessions with the people they've lost – or people pretending to be the people they've lost.'

'The lumps of toadspawn!'

'There's worse,' said the private investigator. 'At the séance you attended, was any financial advice given?'

'Financial advice?' Blotto echoed blankly.

'Was there discussion about stocks and shares? The British Stock Market?'

'Yes, there was some boddo who asked the medium whether he should sell some shares in . . . what was it . . . oh, it's trickled out of the brainbox. Something to do with screws?'

'British Amalgamated Screws?'

'Give that pony a rosette! You've truffled it.'

'And I'll lay any money the questioner was told to sell.'

'You know, Gelatine, you've popped that partridge there too. Exactly what the poor droplet was told to do.'

'It's a racket they're building up all the time. Yes, it starts small, but the news spreads. The kind of people attracted to Aristotours events are often City people. A lot of them are stockbrokers.'

Blotto shuddered. He'd heard about stockbrokers, boddoes who belonged down the bottom of the same sluice-bucket as accountants and solicitors.

'They're attracted to the events,' the private investigator went on, 'because they aspire to the aristocratic life. That's why City people are so keen on all those livery companies, so that they can go through rituals and things as if they had some genuine status in society, whereas in fact they're just what they've always been – middle class!'

Blotto shuddered again, with the instinctive good taste of someone who'd been properly bred.

'Anyway, word goes around from one of these séances that a highly successful company like British Amalgamated Screws is about to go belly-up. These City types start selling, the shares go down to cat's meat prices, whereupon Aristotours operatives buy them up. Then the market readjusts and Aristotours start coining it.'

'Is there no sneakery these four-faced filchers are not capable of?'

'You haven't heard the half of it yet, buddy.' Ivor Gelatine tapped his folder. 'In here are evidence-based accounts of extortion . . . torture . . . murder . . .'

'Murder?' Blotto echoed breathlessly.

'Sure thing. Anyone who gets the wrong side of the Aristotours set-up, anyone who tries to expose their chicanery and—'

The private investigator stopped rather suddenly. Blotto was about to ask him politely to continue when the man toppled down slowly towards him. As he hit the gravel, his fedora fell off. From a small hole in the back of his raincoat, a redness began to spread.

16

Not Again!

Blotto's shocked gaze moved up from Ivor Gelatine's prone body to the frontage of Paramere Castle. At each of the many windows stood one of the Baron's uniformed flunkeys, looking down on him.

Suddenly two of them issued forth from the front doors and, before he had a chance to raise his cricket bat in defence, pinioned Blotto's arms. They chucked his precious weapon unceremoniously into the Lagonda and strong-armed its owner back to Paramere Castle. Somehow, Blotto found he was no longer holding Ivor Gelatine's dossier.

He was bundled into the 'living room' and thrown down in the chair he had so recently vacated. Opposite him, once again, sat a thinly smiling Baron Chipping Norton.

'Not very subtle, Blotto,' he observed.

'Sorry, Chippers, I'm not on the same bus. What do you mean?'

'Committing murder in front of so many witnesses is not the work of a top-rank genius.'

'"Committing murder"? I don't know what you're gabbing on about.'

'No? Do you deny that Ivor Gelatine is dead?'

'No, with you on that one. He does look pretty thoroughly coffinated. Won't be pushing the daisies back down again in a hurry.'

'Fortunately,' said the Baron silkily, 'we have managed to find the murder weapon.'

One of his uniformed flunkeys stepped forward, right on cue, with a familiar-looking revolver. He held it daintily in a handkerchief, so as to minimise contact with its metal surfaces.

'Wonderful,' the Baron went on, 'the way the science of fingerprints is developing these days.'

'Well ...' Blotto chuckled. 'You'll certainly find my spoffing fingerprints on that slug-shifter.'

'That's rather what I thought.'

'But that doesn't mean I coffinated the poor boddo.'

'Doesn't it?'

'No, Chippers me old tin of boiled sweets,' Blotto explained, as to a small child. 'My dabbers got on the shooter when you passed it over to me, very kindly offering it as a means of protection.'

'Sorry? I have no recollection of that happening.'

Blotto chuckled again. 'Then you're a bit of a moist mop on the memory front, Chippers.' He looked around at the assembled flunkeys. 'All these boddoes saw it happen.'

Baron Chipping Norton addressed his staff. 'Did any of you see me hand over this revolver to Lord Devereux Lyminster?'

'No,' replied the assembled flunkeys with one voice.

'So, what did you see?'

For this reply they abandoned unison speech and let one speak for all. 'We saw,' he said gravely, 'this gentleman, Lord Devereux Lyminster, use that revolver to shoot the private investigator, Ivor Gelatine.'

'Oh, puddledash!' said Blotto. 'I only met the poor greengage this morning. What possible reason could I have for coffinating him?'

'I think this might provide the motive,' said Baron Chipping Norton, and he picked up a green folder with the word 'Aristotours' on the front. 'The contents here are pretty explosive stuff and would certainly give you reason to kill to silence the person who compiled them. Maybe you'd like to have a look.'

This time Blotto laughed out loud. 'Oh, Chippers, you have so got the wrong end of the sink plunger! I've seen a bit of the scribbling in that folder. And yes, it's explosive globbins all right, but it's not me it sticks the suckers on. No, if you were pricking the peepers for a motive for *you* to coffinate that poor p. i. pineapple, you'd find it here with three veg and gravy.' He opened the folder. 'I only read the opening salvo, but you lock your lugs on this.'

Confidently, Blotto started to read.

'This dossier contains irrefutable evidence that the Aristotours company is a front for a major criminal enterprise, run from Tawcester Towers by Lord Devereux Lyminster.'

His words trickled away. 'Someone's played a diddler's hand here! They've done a swopsie on the files!'

'If that had happened, Blotto,' said Baron Chipping Norton smoothly, 'one of my staff would have seen the switch.' He turned to them. 'Did any of you witness such an exchange of files take place?'

They reverted to unison for the 'No!'

The Baron fixed Blotto with a steely eye. 'Then I'm afraid it looks as if you're about to be accused of a second murder, with many more witnesses than were present when you stabbed Viscount Washbourne.'

'Chippers, you are so shinnying up the wrong drainpipe. There is an amazingly simple reason why no one could believe that I coffinated the poor Gelatine greengage.'

'And what is that?'

'He was shot in the back.'

'And . . . ?'

Blotto smiled proudly as he produced his clinching argument. 'No Lyminster would ever shoot anyone in the back!'

Strangely, Baron Chipping Norton didn't see that argument as entirely clinching, and Blotto found himself incarcerated

116

in the Paramere Castle dungeon. Unlike the rest of the building, this area had not been modernised to suburban blandness and remained in the state it had been for centuries. Water dripped down the blackened walls, into which the remains of rusty manacles were fixed. The only light came from two small grilles set at ground level, which for the dungeon was ceiling level. Scuttling sounds and occasional squeaks told Blotto that he was sharing his accommodation with a large number of rats.

For some people, this situation would have been regarded as a dispiriting one. Some might even have despaired. But despair was not a word in Blotto's vocabulary (though 'despare', without an 'i' and with an 'e' at the end, was – he had never, as his Eton beaks would testify, been good at spelling).

He knew he'd be all right. He knew he had not killed Ivor Gelatine – or Viscount Washbourne, come to that. And Blotto was sublimely confident in the majesty of British justice, which always found out the truth.

Also, he reckoned he'd fulfilled the mission which had brought him to Paramere Castle. He couldn't wait to share with Twinks the new information he'd gathered about the perfidy of Baron Chipping Norton and his connection to Aristotours.

Huh, let his sister try saying again that he shouldn't conduct investigations on his own!

And, as for being stuck in prison for a while, Lyminsters had endured worse during the Wars of the Roses.

Blotto's imprisonment in the dungeon did not, as it turned out, last very long. Unbeknownst to him, Baron Chipping Norton had put through a phone call immediately after his incarceration, which had resulted in the arrival at Paramere Castle a few hours later of a Black Maria. Inside it were Chief Inspector Trumbull and Sergeant Knatchbull of the

Tawcestershire Constabulary, together with Sir Albert Anstruther, Chief Constable of the county.

After the Inspector had read Blotto his rights and arrested him for the murder of Ivor Gelatine, Bertie Anstruther said, 'You're rather making a habit of this, Lord Devereux.'

17

Durance Vile

Grimshaw the butler escorted the Dowager Duchess with all due ceremony to the telephone in the hall. He then lifted the receiver and gave the required number. A cat may look at a king, but a telephone operator was not allowed to speak directly to a Dowager Duchess. Or, at least, not at Tawcester Towers.

Once Grimshaw had established that Sir Albert Anstruther was on the line, he passed the receiver decorously to his employer.

'Bertie, what in the name of all that's holy is going on with Blotto?'

'Good morning, Your Grace. Lord Devereux Lyminster is being held on remand in Perylgrim.' He referred to the highest security prison in Tawcestershire.

'Perylgrim? Why isn't he being held in Tawsworthy police station?'

'Tawsworthy police station is too easy to escape from.'

'Well, I don't care whether it's Tawsworthy or Perylgrim, Bertie. Get him out of there and back here to Tawcester Towers!'

'I'm afraid that is not possible, Your Grace.'

'Not possible?' The Dowager Duchess rumbled like a volcano thirty seconds before eruption. 'I am telling you to do it, Bertie!'

'Your Grace, I don't think you are aware of the serious-ness of the crimes with which your son is charged.'

'They're only murders, aren't they?' said the Dowager Duchess.

'Yes, but there are two of them.'

'Two, three . . . it doesn't matter how many there are. The point is that Blotto didn't do them.'

'There's a strong body of evidence to suggest that he did.'

'Poo,' said the Dowager Duchess.

'I beg your pardon, Your Grace?'

'Poo,' she repeated. 'Listen, Bertie, I have known you since you were in nip-naps.'

'That is neither here nor there.'

'Oh, it is very much here and there. What's more, I knew your mother before you were born . . .'

'Yes . . .' The confidence in the Chief Constable's voice had crumbled away.

'And I knew the company she kept in those days . . .'

'Ah,' came the uncomfortable response.

'From the nursery onward, Bertie, the likeness was observed between you and a certain dark-haired stableboy who left your father's employ shortly before your birth.'

Silence from the other end of the line.

'Bertie, would you wish me to spread that piece of infor-mation among certain titled ladies of my acquaintance?'

That prompted a little strangled cry. Then the Chief Constable said, the words almost choking him as he formed them, 'I cannot stop you from doing that, Your Grace. But it will not change the fact that your younger son remains in Perylgrim on remand for two murders.'

The Dowager Duchess passed the receiver to Grimshaw. He, knowing from long experience the right thing to do, slammed it down into its cradle with considerable force.

Of course, Blotto's Lagonda was still where he'd left it, on the gravel in front of Paramere Castle. Twinks sent Corky

Froggett off with another chauffeur in one of the Tawcester Towers Rolls-Royces to collect it. They didn't see anyone when they reclaimed the car. They knocked at the modern doors to say what they were doing, but no one answered.

Baron Chipping Norton and his uniformed heavies were either elsewhere or lying low.

Things had moved fast. It was less than a week after the dinner at Clusters when Twinks received through the post a stiff card with gilded lettering. It read:

ARISTOTOURS
INVITE YOU TO FIND OUT
HOW THE OTHER HALF LIVE
OVER AN ARISTOCRATIC WEEKEND
AT TAWCESTER TOWERS
(ANCESTRAL SEAT OF THE DUKES OF TAWCESTER,
THE LYMINSTERS AND SOME FAMILY GHOSTS!)
ENTERTAINMENTS WILL INCLUDE
HUNTING, SHOOTING, FISHING, CRICKET, A SÉANCE
AND MIXING WITH GENUINE ARISTOCRATS
(WHO, INCIDENTALLY, MAY ATTEND THE WEEKEND
WITHOUT PAYMENT).
PRICES AND BOOKING ON APPLICATION BY POST
TO THE MASTER OF THE REVELS
AT TAWCESTER TOWERS.

The filth-fingering slugbuckets! was Twinks's silent reaction. She had anticipated something of the kind as soon as Mr Weissfeder was appointed as Master of the Revels, but not so soon. The event was less than three weeks away. Rodney Perkins would only just have restored hot water to Tawcester Towers.

Twinks was peeved that things had obviously been going on behind her back. Someone must have been working hand-in-glove with Aristotours for quite a while. The same someone must have agreed to license the appalling invasion that Tawcester Towers was about to suffer. And though the event had probably been sanctioned in name by the Duke of Tawcester, she was sure that Loofah had just been the velvet glove encasing the iron fist of their mother.

It wasn't the betrayal of Lyminster family traditions that upset Twinks. She knew the Dowager Duchess for the unsentimental old battleaxe she was. Her mother would go to any lengths to secure the continuity of life at Tawcester Towers. What worried Twinks was the sinister force that lay behind the façade of Aristotours, the Anarchists. They represented the real threat to everything the Lyminster family held dear.

Twinks decided it was time to have another conversation with Professor Erasmus Holofernes.

'How excellent to hear you, my dear Twinks. You anticipated me. I was about to put through a call to Tawcester Towers.'

'Splendissimo, Razzy. Does that mean you've got some new gin-gen?'

'Yes, the information I have unearthed is not as complete as I might wish, but it is nonetheless disturbing. Tell me, have there been any developments for you in connection with Aristotours?'

Quickly, Twinks summarised the background to her brother's latest arrest for murder.

'And is Blotto in distress?'

'Not so far as I can understand, no.'

'You mean he's safely at home with you at Tawcester Towers?'

'No, he's boarded up in a clinkbox called Perylgrim.' The Professor winced audibly. 'Why, is the place a swamphole?'

'It has a reputation for an extremely strict regime – and for being impossible to escape from.'

'We Lyminsters have always liked a challenge,' said

Twinks. Then, remembering, 'But Blotto is not likely to try shedding the shackles on his own. He's quite capable of thinking it's tickey-tockey for him to stay in Perylgrim until his trial.'

'Why on earth would he think that?' asked Holofernes.

'Because, Razzy . . .' Twinks took a deep breath '. . . Blotto has faith in the majesty of British justice.'

'Oh dear,' said the Professor.

'Blotto thinks the fact that he didn't coffinate either of the people he's accused of coffinating means that he will be found not guilty in any British court of law.'

'Oh dear, oh dear,' said the Professor. 'And what kind of a case have his accusers got against him for the second murder?'

Twinks spelled it all out – the fingerprints, the false dossier, and the witness statements of the entire Paramere Castle staff.

'Oh dear, oh dear, oh dear,' said the Professor.

'I'm going to visit Blotters in Perylgrim as soon as possible. See if I can batter some sense into his brainbox about this. Mind you, that's something I've been trying to do since I was in nursery naps . . . without marked success. When it comes to matters of honour, or defending what he regards as British values, Blotto's as stubborn as a bulldog in the butcher's. But don't worry, Razzy,' she concluded confidently, 'I'll make him change his mind.'

'You must get him out, my dear Twinks. The powers behind Aristotours are definitely forces of evil.'

'You've found out more? Come on, uncage the ferrets!'

'It concerns the Crooked Hand. I told you they are an Anarchist organisation devoted to bringing down all of the major institutions in the world.'

'Bong on the nose.'

'Everything more I find out about them only makes matters worse. Their methods involve infinite cruelty. They have no respect for humankind. If they are not stopped, they will destroy the world as we know it!'

123

'Tough little tinkers then,' Twinks observed coolly.

'Yes. But, though I am convinced they are in some way linked up to Aristotours, I cannot for the life of me provide a link between that company and the Secret Congregation of the Crooked Hand.'

'Is that what's on their name-tag, Razzy?'

'Yes, that's the full name of their organisation.'

'Then I can come up with the silverware so far as the connection's concerned.'

'You can?'

'Easy as a housemaid's virtue. You remember I told you about the oilskin wrapper on the false testimony document sent from Baron Chipping Norton to Tawsworthy police station?'

'Yes.'

'And there was a spoffing word on that oilskin.'

'"Scotch".'

Twinks left a pause before her revelation. 'Which stands for the "Secret Congregation of the Crooked Hand". Doesn't it, Razzy?'

'Of course it does! Why didn't I see that? How do you do it?'

'Just a knackette,' said Twinks modestly.

'The Dowager Duchess's anger,' said Corky Froggett, 'was noted below stairs.'

'She's as cross as a wasp in a water-ice,' said Twinks, who had chosen to sit in the front of the Lagonda, next to the chauffeur. From her wrist casually dangled her sequinned reticule. Tawcestershire was looking its best as the Lagonda queened her way through the country lanes. 'Bertie Anstruther, the Chief Constable . . . ' she went on.

'Is he the gentleman, milady, whose father was a stableboy?'

'You're bong on the nose there, Corky. But I thought that particular secret was kept under the dustbin lid.'

'I can assure you, milady,' said Corky, 'that all such information is known to everyone below stairs.'

'Splendissimo,' murmured Twinks who, when she came to think about it, was not really surprised by the revelation. 'Yes, anyway, Bertie, who has never stood up to the Mater before, is sticking to his guns like cow-heel glue. Just because my brother has been accused of two coffinations, the Chief Constable insists on keeping him in the clinkbox.'

'Very short-sighted, milady,' said the chauffeur. 'But, in my experience, entirely characteristic of the constabulary mentality.'

'Yes, more's the moping. I think we're going to need Blotto on the prems for the next few weeks. There's some horracious backdoor-sidling going on at Tawcester Towers. Has below stairs got the semaphore yet about a ghastible invitation Aristotours has issued?'

'It certainly has, milady. And a right load of consternation that has started. Our new Master of the Revels has already caused a lot of ruffled feathers among the kitchen maids. And he's been downright rude to the chef about the food he's producing. The extra changes Mr Weissfeder wants implemented before the weekend when all the riff-raff are coming to Tawcester Towers are making him even more unpopular. It's getting to such a pitch that Grimshaw was almost seen to frown.'

'That bad, huh? Anyway, I think we need Blotters on the strength for whatever fumacious thimble-jiggling lies ahead. Do you reckon we can spring him from Perylgrim?'

'Undoubtedly, milady. That is, if he's willing to be sprung.'

'What do you mean? Blotters doesn't want to spend the rest of his bornies in a clinkbox.'

'I'm sure he doesn't, milady. However, the young master does suffer from some unfortunate beliefs.'

'"Unfortunate beliefs"? What? Come on, Corky, uncage the ferrets.'

And so the chauffeur told Twinks about his unsuccessful attempt to spring her brother from Tawsworthy police station.

'Oh, snickets!' she said. 'I didn't realise the sit was as bad as that. The bro still has faith in the majesty of British justice?'

'That would appear to be the case, milady.'

'Rodents!'

'Yes, it is unfortunate, milady.'

'It's absolutely the baboon's elbow, Corky. Don't don your worry-boots, though.'

'You think you'll be able to change the young master's opinion?'

'Is the King German?' asked Twinks, with a confident grin.

18

A Lesson from History

There were strict rules about visiting at Perylgrim Prison. Permission had to be obtained at Chief Constable level and a date could rarely be fixed at less than a month's notice. No one could just drop in unannounced one afternoon.

Unless, of course, that person was Lady Honoria Lyminster. The most rigid of regulations had a tendency to melt in the rays from her azure eyes.

Under their gaze, the iron determination of the guards on Perylgrim's main gates turned quickly to overcooked cabbage. And Twinks found herself straight away escorted to the office of the Prison Governor.

This individual was called Craig Cragston, which was entirely appropriate because, in a World Open Cragginess Competition, he could have given the Dowager Duchess of Tawcester a run for her money. He was scarily muscular, but the only muscles he'd never used were the ones that made smiles.

He was also not very tall. When he rose from his desk at Twinks's entrance, he was shorter than she was. Which, for a man, was quite short. His autocratic, peppery manner suggested to his visitor, who had read deeply in the newly discovered discipline of psychology, that he might be afflicted by what is known as the 'Napoleon Complex'.

This, supposedly, led short men to overcompensate by autocratic behaviour.

Within the prison service, Governor Cragston had built up a daunting reputation for the harshness of the regimes he imposed. He was such a stern disciplinarian that his staff were as frightened of him as the prisoners were. Many convicted murderers spent their time between conviction and execution at Perylgrim, and there was anecdotal evidence that, compared to those weeks, what happened on the gallows was reckoned to be getting off lightly. Some authorities were even of the view that the reputation of Craig Cragston had caused a considerable decline in the country's murder statistics. Jealous husbands and black-mail victims, about to strike the fatal blow, remembered him and thought better of it.

Craig Cragston was also a fervent Socialist, deeply offended by elitism and firmly of the view that the aristocracy should be abolished.

His office was dark institutional green, with no furniture but his desk, adorned only by a telephone, and three chairs. The walls were innocent of decoration, save for one portrait of a stern, bushy-eyebrowed man in nineteenth-century military uniform.

'So,' the Prison Governor, now seated, boomed over his desk at Twinks, 'what on earth makes you think I should make an exception to Perylgrim's visiting regulations for you? If you imagine that I would be impressed by your title and family history, then you're very definitely knock-ing on the wrong door.'

'Oh, I'm on the same bus with you there,' said Twinks. 'I don't believe in special privilege for any poor pineapple, regardless of their background,' she added, lying through her teeth. Then, laying it on with a butter-knife, she quoted John Ball from the 1381 Peasant's Revolt, '"When Adam delved and Eve span, Who was then the gentleman"?'

'Exactly,' said Cragston. But any advance Twinks hoped

to have gained was negated by his next words. 'So, you agree that I shouldn't change the regulations for you?'

'Well, rein in the roans a moment there,' she said. Slowly, she hitched up the hem of her short skirt, revealing a further expanse of white-stockinged leg, and focused on the Prison Governor the flash from those azure eyes that had enslaved amorous swains from Moscow to Manhattan.

The unaltered cragginess of Craig Cragston's expression instantly demonstrated his immunity to feminine wiles, so she put hers away and moved to a more promising line of attack.

She looked up at the portrait on the wall, whose subject she had, of course, instantly identified. (It was fortunate that recently her insatiable curiosity had led to her doing some research into the Napoleonic period.) 'Beezer news,' Twinks said coolly, 'that you unfurl the flag for General Sir Hudson Lowe.'

It had been the right approach. The craggy jaw dropped. 'You mean you recognise him?'

'Bong on the nose, Governor. I too have worshipped him since I was in nursery nip-naps.'

'By jingo!' said Cragston. 'It's so rare for me to meet anyone who even knows who he was. I have tried to interest the prison officers here at Perylgrim in the career of General Sir Hudson Lowe, but without success. They suffer from a complete lack of intellectual curiosity about Sir Hudson . . . as well as most other subjects. And yet . . . you know about him?'

'Tickey-tockey.' Twinks smiled knowledgably. 'Hard to dab the digit on anyone who had better qualiffs to keep Napoleon in the clinkbox.'

'You are so right.' There was something approaching enthusiasm in the Prison Governor's voice. 'General Sir Hudson Lowe has, for me, always been the archetype of what the custodian of important prisoners should be. His is an example which I have tried diligently to emulate throughout my own career in the service.'

'And I'm sure, in that respect, you've really won the raffle. It was just pure creamy éclair,' Twinks went on, 'that Lowe was given the jobbo of custodian of Napoleon on St Helena on the first of August 1815 . . .'

'I couldn't agree more.'

'. . . though, of course, he didn't actually arrive on St Helena till April the fourteenth 1816 . . .'

'No.'

'. . . having only a month before married Susan Delancey Johnson, daughter of Colonel Stephen Delancey and widow of Colonel William Johnson who'd been killed in 1811 in battle with the French . . .'

'Lady Honoria,' said Cragston, momentarily forgetting his anti-elitist principles, 'I never expected to meet anyone who shared to such a degree my enthusiasm for the career of General Sir Hudson Lowe as the supreme jailer of Napoleon.'

'Oh, I've had the wiggles for him all my bornies,' said Twinks. Then, casually, 'Why don't we continue our chittle-chattle about him while we go and visit my brother . . . ?'

Twinks counted the doors Craig Cragston led her through before she was allowed to greet Blotto. Three . . . well, four, including the main gates by which she had entered the prison, each with more locks and bolts than the previous one.

But she didn't let the level of security dispirit her. She felt confident that she and Corky, perhaps with some technical advice from Professor Erasmus Holofernes, could easily spring Blotto from Perylgrim. She consigned the details of each lock into separate compartments of her photographic memory, so that she would know what equipment to bring in her sequinned reticule for her next visit to the prison.

As the Governor escorted her to her destination, Twinks kept up lively banter about how Hudson Lowe had joined the regiment of his father John, the 50th Foot; how, after the Peace of Amiens in 1803 he had been appointed assistant quartermaster-general; how in 1809 he had become Governor of Cephalonia, Ithaca and Santa Maura . . .

In the visiting room, the siblings were separated by a wide table, but they wouldn't have hugged or anything, anyway. Boddoes and breath-sappers of their breeding didn't go in for hugging, as a rule – certainly not when they were brother and sister. The upbringing decreed by the Dowager Duchess and administered by a sequence of nursemaids and governesses had not involved physical contact.

Craig Cragston said he would leave them alone to talk, but insisted that, before she left Perylgrim, Lady Honoria should go back to his office for further discussion of General Sir Hudson Lowe's career.

After the minimal pleasantries of greeting, Twinks got straight down to business. 'Listen, Blotters me old sardine on toast,' she said, 'we've got to get you out of this treacle tin.'

'Twinks me old darning needle, it's no skin off my rice pudding,' said Blotto.

'But this Prison Governor is supposed to be as tough as a rhino's rump.'

Blotto shrugged. 'Seems all tickey-tockey. Warders are quite amiable boddoes, food's marginally better than it was at Eton. I'm not being rubber-banded on the rack or anything like that. Miss chewing the breeze with Mephistopheles – and cricket, of course – but I'm certainly not down the stickiest end of the paint pot. And it won't be for ever.'

'You mean you're hoping soon to be as free as a seed in a puffball?'

'Bong on the nose, Twinkers. Not hoping, though – certain. I'll be back at Tawcester Towers in no time.'

'The thought hasn't occurred to you, Blotters, that you might be found guilty?'

'No.'

'Why not?'

'Because I'm not guilty.'

Faced by such naïve good faith, Twinks's eyes rolled heavenwards. 'Because,' she asked sarcastically, 'you believe in the majesty of British justice?'

'Another bong bang on the bridge!' Blotto beamed. 'So, don't don your worry-boots about trying to get me out of here. I'll stand trial and then I'll be out, quick as a lizard's lick . . . thanks to the majesty of British justice.'

'And you believe that British justice always gets things right?'

'Of course. The only kind of boddo who'd say otherwise is a stencher from abroad-land.'

'Blotto, might I give you an example from history?'

His brow clouded. 'Bit of an empty revolver when it comes to history,' he said. 'Or at least, that's what the beaks at Eton were always telling me.'

'This bit of history concerns the Lyminster family.'

His brow cleared. 'Tickey-tockey,' he said.

'Now, Blotters, you remember the English Civil War . . . ?'

'Well,' he replied cautiously, 'not jereboamsful of detail about it. Bit before my time, wasn't it?'

'You've potted the black there, Blotters. And, just to sprinkle a bit of memory dust, may I remind you that the two sides in the English Civil War were the Roundheads . . .'

'Oikish sponge-worms with short hair and no breeding?'

'That's the Johnnies. Cromwell's New Model Army.'

'Bit of a rum baba. I remember thinking when one of the beaks at Eton first mentioned it. You'd have thought this Cromwell boddo would have stood a better chance with a full-size army than a model one.'

Twinks let that go into the net without comment. 'So, you had the oikish Roundheads on one side, and on the other—'

'The Caviars!' Blotto announced triumphantly.

'I think "Cavaliers" is the wordette you're looking for,' suggested Twinks.

'Give that pony a rosette! And the Cavaliers were definitely our kind of people. Long-haired, dashing, got lots of derring-do derring-done, I remember.'

'Grandissimo! And, Blotters, can you dab a digit on who was Duke of Tawcester during the English Civil War?'

'He was called Rupert,' Blotto replied confidently. That was the easy bit of the question. Every Duke of Tawcester since the Norman Conquest had been called Rupert. Loofah's first name was also inescapably Rupert, though nobody ever called him that. Over the centuries, some Dukes had had descriptive additions attached to the simple Rupert, according to their character. More colourful examples included Black Rupert, Rupert the Fiend, Rupert the Libertine and Rupert the Dull. The jury of his peers was still out on how Loofah would be remembered by posterity, but the shrewd money was on 'Rupert the Insipid'.

It was no surprise, therefore, that Twinks's follow-up question should be: 'Rupert the what?'

'Rupert the Long-Haired . . . ?' Blotto hazarded.

'No, a much easier rusk to chew,' said his sister. 'He was called Rupert the Cavalier.'

'Good ticket. I think there's a daub of him in the Long Gallery.'

'There is indeed. And it's almost recovered from when you and your old muffin-toasters from Eton threw cream buns at it.'

Blotto smiled fondly at the recollection. 'I may not know much about art,' he said, 'but I do like throwing food at it.'

'Anyway . . .' Twinks needed to get to the point. 'Rupert the Cavalier was a Grade A foundation stone.'

'With three veg and gravy!' Blotto agreed.

'But do you know why he unsheathed his sabre in the English Civil War?'

133

'To stop the country being taken over by Cromwell's tin soldiers. He didn't want the place overrun by accountants and solicitors and Socialists. He wanted the right sort of people to be back where they should be – in charge.'

'That was part of the reason, yes, Blotters. But it was also to avenge an act of regicide.' There was a silence. 'Does "regicide" mean anything to you, Blotto?'

'Not sure. There are a couple of chumboes I know at the Gren . . .' The Grenadiers, his London club '. . . brothers called Dickey and Bobby Side. There may be a third bro called Reggie Side, but I haven't clapped my peepers on him.'

'No,' said his sister patiently. 'Regicide is killing a King.'

'That's way beyond the barbed wire!'

'It certainly is.'

'Kind of rombooley that wooky lot the other side of the Channel got up to. With their French Rev. And their galantine.'

'Guillotine,' Twinks corrected gently. 'Anyway, we were first to the fence on that one.'

'Not on the same page, sis?'

'Long before the French Rev, Charles the First got neck-knackered.'

'I'd forgotten. So he did, by Denzil. Poor droplet,' Blotto concluded piously.

'And why, in the name of strawberries, do you think that happened?'

'Because Cromwell and his Pinheads—'

'Roundheads.'

'Tickey-tockey. Anyway, they wanted to destroy all civilisation. Like the Antichrists.'

'Anarchists.'

'Them, yes.'

'In fact, Blotters, in spite of the support of boddoes like our ancestor Rupert the Cavalier, Charles the First was found guilty in a trial.'

'A trial where?'

'In the High Court of Justice.'

'And what's that when it's got its spats on?'

'A court of law. It is, in fact, an example of the majesty of British justice.'

'And it was the majesty of British justice that had Charles the First blockchopped?'

'Certainly was, Blotters.'

'Well, I'll be battered like a pudding!' There was a silence while he took in the ramifications of this. Then, 'How soon can you get me out of this clinkbox, Twinks?'

19

Plumbers and Planners

In the Lagonda on the way back, Twinks heard more from Corky Froggett about the disruption below stairs caused by Mr Weissfeder's appointment. The Master of the Revels was contriving to rub everyone up the wrong way. Even those of the domestic staff who'd initially liked the idea of the 'How The Other Half Live' weekend were now as firmly against it as Twinks herself.

She did not at that point mention to Corky her plans to spring Blotto from Perylgrim. Before doing that, she needed to make more detailed preparations. Nor did she tell him that she'd finally managed to wean her brother off his blind faith in the majesty of British justice. She knew that when the call came, she would be able to rely totally on the chauffeur's loyalty and support.

On her return to Tawcester Towers, Twinks tried to talk to her mother, but the Dowager Duchess was incommunicado. Her personal maid said she was not to be disturbed. This was a frequently used ploy. When there was something she did not wish to discuss, the matriarch would just put herself out of circulation. Nobody argued with that. It was one of the privileges of being a Dowager Duchess.

What she didn't wish to discuss on this occasion was, her

daughter knew full well, her association with Aristotours and the 'How The Other Half Live' invitation.

So Twinks decided she might see how things were proceeding in the refurbishment of Tawcester Towers' heating system.

Though members of Rodney Perkins's work team were seen all around the great house, installing radiators in the far-flung wings, running pipes and electrical wires under ancestral floorboards, the plumber himself spent most of his time in the cellar. There it was that the ancient behemoth of a coal-fired boiler was being replaced by something more modern.

The gleaming new boiler dominated a large amount of technical equipment scattered throughout the extensive cellars of Tawcester Towers. A confusion of piping, tool-boxes, reels of electrical wire and other impedimenta of unknown function littered the stone flooring.

Twinks had, as she had of most things, an intuitive understanding of heating systems and, on inspecting the gleaming new boiler, asked where you put the coal in.

'Ah,' said Rodney Perkins, 'that is how these new devices are so revolutionary. They don't use coal.'

'Great spangled spiders!' said Twinks. 'Then what do they use?'

The plumber pointed to a long row of drums against the cellar wall. 'Welcome, milady, to the future. No chopping down of forests involved, no shovelling, no ash to remove, no noxious fumes. The future is . . . oil.'

'Isn't oil a tidge volatile?' asked Twinks. 'Isn't there a riskette of fire?'

'No more than there is in an internal combustion engine. You feel safe in your brother's Lagonda, don't you?'

Twinks had to confess that she did.

'Well, there's no more risk in one of these boilers than there is in the car.'

'Splendissimo,' murmured Twinks. 'And what your boddoes are all round T.T. laying pipes for . . . is a radiator system?'

'Exactly. You're on the money there.'

She looked back at the drums lined up against the wall. 'You seem to need jereboamsful of oil, don't you?'

'Hungry beast, that boiler,' he said quickly. 'But there are huge advantages to an oil-fired system. No more bedroom fireplaces. Heating in every room in the house, all controlled from this boiler here.'

'Heaven on a pickle-fork,' said Twinks. Though she'd heard of such things happening in mansions the other side of the Atlantic, the idea of every room in an English stately home being warm was beyond even her imagination. Chilblains were considered an essential part of the country house weekend. As were damp sheets.

That thought reminded her of the 'How The Other Half Live' invitation. 'So, Mr Perkins, will you have all these flipmadoodles in readiness for the weekend after this?'

'That's the plan, milady.'

'Good ticket. Have you heard about the horracious jamboree happening then?'

'Hard to avoid the subject, milady. Nobody below stairs is talking about anything else.'

'That's no jawdropper. Poor thimbles, their lives are being totally crabwhacked by it.'

'So it seems. I gather, milady, you are not an enthusiast for the projected event?'

'You can say that again with two veg and gravy!'

'And might I hazard,' the plumber asked humbly, 'that your objection is the thought of your ancestral home being invaded by people of inferior breeding . . . ?'

'You've dabbed the digit on it there, Mr Perkins. There is a long tradition amongst people of our sort allowing oikish sponge-worms to pay a shilling and inspect our gardens . . . even have a look at some of the more formal rooms inside the prems . . . but this Aristotours plan is way the wrong side of wrong. The suggestion that these lumps of toadspawn should pay money to mingle with the aristocracy ... well, that is definitely outside the rule book.'

'So,' asked the plumber thoughtfully, 'which aristocrats will these undesirables be meeting at the weekend?'

'Sadly, we Lyminsters can't duck under the drapery on this one. The Mater will see to that – though she is quite capable of hiding in the hedgerow herself. So, it'll be me and my two bros who get wheeled out ... that's the Duke and Blotto ... Oh, and Loofah's wife Sloggo.'

'And you will not be asking others of similar breeding to your own to join you, milady?'

'Great whiffling water rats, no! It's bad enough us having to suffer, we don't want to put lumps in our chumboes' custard.'

'I was just thinking, milady, of a rather odd detail in the Aristotours' "How The Other Half Live" invitation ...'

'Oh? And what's that when it's got its spats on?'

'It says that aristocrats do not have to pay for the event.'

'Well, that would be adding sneering to suffering. We don't want our chumboes to know anything about this weekend; we'll keep the whole thing under the candle-snuffer.'

'But I was just thinking, milady,' Rodney Perkins began slowly, 'there might be a way you could get one over on Aristotours ...'

'How? Come on, uncage the ferrets!'

'Well, presumably Aristotours will be paying the costs of the whole weekend?'

'Yes, and no doubt overcharging the participants and taking all the profits, like the four-faced filchers that they are.'

'Mm ...' The plumber rubbed his chin thoughtfully. 'But suppose, rather than keeping quiet about the weekend, you were to invite every member of the aristocracy that you know ... ?'

'Never in a donkey's millennium!' said Twinks proudly.

'If you were to do that,' Perkins persisted, 'and fill all of the available places with genuine aristocrats, then there wouldn't be any space left for ... the wrong sort of people you're so worried about, and you would be able to entertain all your friends to a lavish weekend of entertainment ... at the expense of Aristotours.'

Twinks looked at the plumber with new respect. 'Give that pony an extremely large rosette!' she said.

She sought out the Duke in his East Wing. After wading through a morass of small daughters, she found him in his study, looking as vacant as ever. Loofah, in fact, wore his customary look of a door whose sign will never read 'engaged'.

Twinks had no idea how her elder brother filled his time. She had a feeling he probably spent the daylight hours looking out of the window of his study, before hauling himself off at bedtime for more doomed conjugal duties.

'Erm ...' he said, predictably enough, on her arrival in his study. It was as bare as ever, no Napoleonic portraits on his walls.

'Loofah me old bootscraper,' said Twinks, 'I've just had a real bellbuzzer of an idea about this horracious weekend that's louring over the horizon.'

'Erm ...' The Duke claimed not to know what she was talking about. This was not unusual. He rarely knew what anyone was talking about.

Patiently, Twinks spelled out the idea that Rodney Perkins had planted in her mind, that they should invite all of their aristocratic friends to the 'How The Other Half Live' weekend and thus keep Tawcester Towers free of oikish sponge-worms.

Still, Loofah didn't get it.

Or at least he claimed not to get it. Twinks suspected that he was playing dumber than he actually was (not an easy feat). And that his real fear was the Dowager Duchess's reaction if he were to spoil the happy relationship she had formed with Aristotours.

Later, she rang Erasmus Holofernes at St Raphael's to discuss General Sir Hudson Lowe. Of course, the Professor knew all about Napoleon's jailer. And yes, he had got some books with illustrations relevant to the man and his career. He said he would have no trouble in discharging the task which Twinks requested.

The goods would be in the post the following day.

20

To The Rescue – Again!

As the 'How The Other Half Live' weekend drew closer, the level of disruption within Tawcester Towers grew exponentially. On top of the laying of pipes and cables for Rodney Perkins's great heating project, major refurbishment of the guest bedrooms was also under way, overseen by the charmless Master of the Revels, Mr Weissfeder. An army of decorators and interior designers invaded the ancestral home, working their transformations at astonishing speed. Décor was changed, mildewed curtains and sagging mattresses were replaced, threadbare sheets and coverlets gave way to crisp new Egyptian cotton.

When Twinks raised with her mother the delicate question of who was paying for all of this, she received, together with a sly grin from the Dowager Duchess, the answer that all expenses were being covered by Aristotours.

This knowledge did not bring Twinks quite the same level of reassurance. It suggested that Aristotours would not be ploughing so much investment into a single weekend. The lumps of toadspawn had longer-term plans. They intended to use Tawcester Towers as a venue for an ongoing series of events. They were planning to turn the ancestral seat of the Lyminsters into something which differed only in detail from an hotel.

What was more, they were doing it with the connivance – not to say enthusiastic support – of the Dowager Duchess of Tawcester.

Twinks felt that these developments had definitely pitched the crud into the crumpets – and must somehow be stopped.

She focused her mighty intellect on the problem.

It would not be true to say that Corky Froggett had never been inside a lady's boudoir. In a lifetime which had encompassed a surprising number of encounters with the fairer sex, he had shared some pleasing months with a couturier called Madame Clothilde of Mayfair, whose boudoir had been as elegant as her sartorial creations.

But the chauffeur had never been inside Twinks's boudoir. Nor, to give him his due, would he ever have expected to do so. Corky Froggett knew his place.

Still, the summons had come. Twinks's personal maid had found him down at the garages on the Tuesday morning before the 'How The Other Half Live' weekend. He had just completed the final duster flick on the Lagonda's gleaming chromium nose. The maid asked him to attend her mistress in her boudoir as soon as possible.

If Corky was surprised by this, he did not allow himself to show it. He had shared enough daredevil adventures with Twinks and her brother to know that she was an unconventional, *modern* young woman. She was rumoured to make cocoa for herself without intervention of domestic staff and had, on more than one occasion, been seen to smoke a cigarette. With Twinks, the normal conventions of interaction between above and below stairs did not apply.

Corky knocked meekly on the door and was granted admission. He did not pass comment on the sophistication of the boudoir (until Mr Weissfeder's recent ministrations, the only room in Tawcester Towers that had any). He just stood inside the closed door, as firmly to attention, each individual hair of his moustache bristling, as he would have, had his Commanding Officer been about to inspect.

From her silk-upholstered seat in front of her silk-draped dressing table, Twinks greeted him. 'Morning, Corky me old mole wrench. Splendiferous to see you!'

'The honour is all mine, milady.'

'Didn't gab about it when we were pongling back in the Lag from Perylgrim, but while I was there, I did bring Blotters' head round to the thoughtette that the majesty of British justice might not always be shouting his name from the touchlines.'

'Congratulations, milady. How on earth did you manage that?'

'Wasn't too tough a rusk to chew, Corky. Trundled him through a bit of Lyminster family history.'

'Always a sensible approach, milady. So, does this mean the young master is no longer content to sit in prison and await his trial?'

'Give that pony a rosette!'

'Are we going to spring him from Perylgrim?' asked the chauffeur eagerly.

'We are indeed! I just needed to get my skittles into sequence. Now we're ready for the off.'

'Excellent, milady!'

'But I won't be able to do the springing without you on the team, Corky.'

'As ever, milady, anything involving you or the young master commands my unswerving loyalty.'

'Splendissimo, Corkers!'

'Tell me, will this exploit require my laying my life down for the young master?' he asked hopefully.

'Only if we sabotage our own stratagems.'

'Oh,' said a disappointed Corky.

'If my planette does the business, we'll all three get out without a stain on a single sock.'

'Very good, milady,' said Corky, quickly reconciling himself to the lack of mortal peril.

'Now,' said Twinks, 'some of the wodjermabits we need for my wheezette to work haven't arrived yet. A messenger's even now pongling in this direction from Oxford with them. But . . .' She unhooked her sequinned reticule from the arm of her chair and placed it on the dressing table '. . . everything else we'll need for the Blotto-springing I have right here.'

'Excellent, milady.'

'Come closer, Corky, and I'll explain exactly what your part in the pantomime is . . .'

It was later that afternoon that the consignment Twinks had been expecting arrived at Tawcester Towers. One of the junior porters at St Raphael's College had got quite used to ferrying stuff around the country for Professor Erasmus Holofernes. Such missions were a lot more fun than his usual tasks of pandering to the whims of nit-picking elderly dons. He also got the chance to use the St Raphael's College truck and often juggled the schedule so that he could take his girlfriend out for a drive in it after he'd done the job. His girlfriend had rather strict parents and, since St Raphael's did not admit women, any time the two young people could spend alone in the truck's cab was extremely valuable to them.

So, a jaunt into the beautiful countryside of Tawcester-shire was more than welcome to the porter. Holofernes had made a rare descent from his rooms for punctilious personal supervision of the truck's loading. There had been a large mahogany box with a brass handle on the top and four smaller boxes. The contents of the latter were, as the Professor kept saying, extremely fragile. Before allowing the porter to drive off, he checked twice that the individual items were sufficiently well cushioned to avoid breakages on the bumpy country roads between Oxford and Tawcester Towers.

Professor Erasmus Holofernes would not normally have shown such concern. When he sent off consignments of research to other clients (amongst whom were numbered most of the crowned heads of Europe), he rarely stirred from his desk. But, for Twinks, everything had to be perfect.

Grimshaw had been alerted to the expected arrival of the St Raphael's truck, and it was the butler himself who escorted the heavily laden porter from the front door to Twinks's boudoir.

The young man didn't show the same restraint as Corky Froggett. He gaped open-mouthed at the white silk and lace refinement of the room. When he looked at Twinks herself, goggle eyes joined the open mouth. He had the disloyal thought that he'd prefer it to be Twinks rather than his girlfriend with whom he'd be spending time in the truck's cab when he got back to Oxford.

But he realised that even to entertain such thoughts crossed far too many lines of social convention.

As instructed, he repeated for his hostess the detailed lesson to which he'd been subjected by Professor Erasmus Holofernes in his rooms. He showed her how to undo the brass clasps of the large box and lift the apparatus out. He showed her where the matches and the reservoir of extra oil were stowed.

And he demonstrated the proper way of handling the delicate contents of the other four boxes. As advised by Professor Holofernes, they did two trial runs using the equipment, first with the porter operating it, and then with Twinks doing the job herself.

By the time her visitor left the boudoir, Twinks knew as much about the equipment as he did. And, being of considerably higher intelligence, she had extrapolated a lot more about its workings. Alone in her room, she continued to practise until she had attained an enviable proficiency and felt ready to operate the equipment in front of an audience.

In the truck on the way back to Oxford, the St Raphael's porter felt disconsolate. And though, once there, he did get to spend time in the cab with his girlfriend, the woman who haunted his imagination was not her but the Lady Honoria Lyminster.

Twinks left her boudoir for the hall telephone and asked the operator to put her through to Perylgrim Prison. The Governor was delighted by her suggestion and readily agreed to everything she proposed.

The following afternoon, with Corky Froggett driving and the young mistress in the passenger seat beside him, Blotto's stately Lagonda set off from Tawcester Towers to Perylgrim Prison.

21

Lantern Jaw

'Thank you, Mr Cragston,' said Twinks, 'for that very generous introduction. And welcome to all of you, gentlemen. My name is the Lady Honoria Lyminster, and, at the request of your Governor, I am here this evening to give you a Jaw on a subject very close to his heart.'

She looked out over the crowded audience in what was called the Recreation Room (though the harsh regime imposed by the Governor of Perylgrim left its prisoners little opportunity for recreation). The warders all had their backs to her. So, now, did the Prison Governor. Having concluded his introduction, he had taken a seat in the front row. The only light came from the reflection on the stretched white sheet of the beam from Professor Erasmus Holofernes's magic lantern.

The room was full to the rafters. The Perylgrim staff had not been given the option of missing the lecture. Craig Cragston, stung by his men's previous lack of interest in the man he regarded as the archetype of what a jailer should be, had insisted that all his warders should attend. They had much to learn about the General who oversaw the imprisonment of Napoleon on St Helena for five years.

Twinks was relieved not to be facing her audience. Her brief acquaintance with the Perylgrim warders had shown them to be men without sophistication. And she had already experienced quite enough pop-eyed tongue-lolling and drooling to last her a lifetime.

Also, her position beside Corky Froggett at the back of the room was very much part of her planning for the event. Corky had brought the equipment into Perylgrim and set it up. The St Raphael's magic lantern was not the most modern of machines. It was rarely used at the college, and then only to illustrate lectures in natural science, a discipline whose dons were rather looked down on by the rest of the Senior Common Room. The only proper subject for an academic at Oxford remained Classics.

The latest, most up-to-date, projectors had arc lamps powered by electricity. The St Raphael's model, a beautiful artefact in mahogany and brass, still used light from an oil lamp, reflected in a concave mirror. This did not give as strong a beam as the modern versions and was prone to flickering. Both of which shortcomings suited Twinks's plans perfectly.

Before the audience came into the Recreation Room, Corky had lit and adjusted the wick of the lamp, whose thin radiance would project the slides on to the opposite wall. He had then focused the lens and checked the picture quality with a couple of practice slides. So, when she was introduced, Twinks had described him as the magic lantern's operator. It was the chauffeur therefore, Craig Cragston and the rest of their audience would assume, who would be changing the slides on the cues from his employer's script.

And that, indeed, was what Corky Froggett did. For the first few.

Professor Holofernes had prepared the slides with great care, following Twinks's detailed instructions. There was a photographer in Oxford who had done similar jobs for him before. The expert had captured images from the illustrations the Professor indicated and reproduced them on glass.

The first slide, cued in by Twinks and projected by Corky Froggett, was of a small country town.

'This,' Twinks announced, 'is Galway in Ireland, where Hudson Lowe was born 1769. His mother was Irish and his father, John Lowe, was an army surgeon . . . '

She made no attempt to imbue her narrative with animation. However dull the presentation, Craig Cragston would, of course, focus his highest level of concentration on his favourite subject. The more stupefied the rest of the audience were, so far as Twinks was concerned, the better.

Corky Froggett had just slotted in the third slide, of Salisbury, where the young Hudson Lowe went to school, when he received the agreed nod from the young mistress. After she had handed her sequinned reticule across to him, he slipped silently out of the back of the Recreation Room.

Twinks droned on, 'At the age of eleven, Hudson Lowe was gazetted an ensign in the East Devon Militia . . .'

If there was one thing Corky Froggett was good at, it was following orders. That ability had seen him through the recent little dust-up with the Hun and stood him in good stead in his career at Tawcester Towers. So, when the orders were as clear and detailed as those the young mistress had given him, there was no way he could go wrong.

He remembered every move that they had rehearsed in her boudoir and put them into practice now he was inside Perylgrim.

On leaving the Recreation Room, he turned left and followed a corridor along until he was faced with the first of three internal doors.

The lock on this one, as Twinks had observed on her previous visit, was a Dutton Excelsior Number 4. Corky reached into the sequinned reticule, produced the relevant picklock, and let himself through.

Along the next corridor, he passed rows of cell doors. He couldn't tell whether they were occupied or not; no sound came from within. (In fact, all did contain prisoners but, such was the strictness of the regime inside Perylgrim, none of them dared to make a sound. And none of them had yet realised that there were no warders on duty on the corridors.)

'. . . as can be seen in the next slide . . .'

Adeptly, Twinks removed the one before and slotted in the next image. The rocky outcrops of Corsica appeared on the screen.

'And it was here,' she droned on, 'that Lowe took command of a battalion called the Royal Corsican Rangers, whose ranks were made up of . . .'

In spite of their Governor's presence, individual snores rose from the assembled warders.

The next lock, a Dinkley-Anderson Irontight 237, yielded to the relevant picklock from the sequinned reticule and Corky Froggett advanced to the corridor on which the young master's cell was situated.

Another slide clicked into place and the screen was filled with yet another portrait.

'Swedish by birth,' Twinks intoned, 'this gentleman fought for the Prussian army and became their Field Marshal during the Napoleonic Wars. Gebhard Leberecht von Blücher, Fürst von Wahlstatt, praised the gallantry of General Sir Hudson Lowe after the battle of . . .'

The snoring of the warders had now taken on a rhythmic unity. The whole Recreation Room snored as one (except of course for Craig Cragston, who remained oblivious to the ambient noise, hearing only the fascinating content of Twinks's 'Jaw').

* * *

The last of the picklocks from the sequinned reticule made short work of the Gordon-Bashleigh-Crewe Safefast JWB127 which kept Corky Froggett's young master incarcerated.

Blotto was delighted, but unsurprised, by the chauffeur's appearance in his cell.

'Good ticket, Corky!' he said. 'Knew you'd somehow come up with the silverware.'

'Well, it wasn't just me, milord. Your sister did play a part in planning this rescue.'

'Twinks is a Grade A foundation stone. She has a digit in all the dishiest pies. Where is the old aspidistra now?'

'I think, milord, it would make sense for me to answer that as we make our way back to the Lagonda. We need to make our exit as speedily as possible.'

'Tickey-tockey, Corkers!'

So, the chauffeur retraced his steps, taking the young master through the Gordon-Bashleigh-Crewe Safefast JWB127, the Dinkley-Anderson Irontight 237 and the Dutton Excelsior Number 4. Punctiliously, he relocked each door after them, so that the alarm would not be raised too quickly.

They found the front gates of Perylgrim Prison had been left open, saving Corky the necessity of using the picklock which Twinks had prepared for their Baynes-Woodruff Steeltrap 01896KL.

Soon, Corky Froggett had Blotto safely installed in the sanctuary of the Lagonda's dickey, where he was delighted to be reunited with his cricket bat.

'. . . and this is Charlotte Cottage . . .' Twinks had just clicked the last slide into the magic lantern as Corky sidled into the back of the Recreation Room to join her. 'It is near Sloane Street in Chelsea, and it was there that General Sir Hudson Lowe died of paralysis on the tenth of January 1844.

'Thank you all so much for listening to my Jaw. I do hope you've enjoyed it.'

Corky switched the lights back on and all the warders tried to give the impression they'd been awake throughout the whole proceedings.

Craig Cragston was fulsome in his praise of Twinks's lecture. 'I cannot imagine Hudson Lowe's story being more dramatically or comprehensively told, Lady Honoria. And I can't thank you enough for what this will have done for my men. They now have another exemplar, apart from myself, to demonstrate to them the highest standards of the prison service.'

The Governor insisted that some of his warders should help carry the magic lantern equipment out to the Lagonda. They were about to put it in the dickey, but Twinks suggested they leave that locked and place their burden on the back seat.

Then Corky set off to drive the Lagonda back to Tawcester Towers.

A couple of miles away from Perylgrim, he stopped at the roadside. Blotto left the cramped quarters of the dickey for the familiar comfort of the driving seat. Corky sat in the back.

And, as they roared through the beauties of the Tawcestershire countryside, knocking bicycling vicars into the hedgerows with wild abandon, Blotto and Twinks agreed that the whole escapade had been 'pure creamy éclair'.

22

Two Heads Better Than One?

Blotto was ecstatic to be back at Tawcester Towers. 'I'm rolling on camomile lawns, Twinks me old banana-peeler!' he enthused to his sister as the stately Lagonda turned into the long gravelled drive.

Blissfully reunited with his cricket bat and Lagonda, Blotto still had one more love affair to pursue. As soon as he'd brought the car to a halt outside Tawcester Towers' main doors, he went straight to the stables to commune with Mephistopheles. He spent a surprisingly long time down there. Man and horse had a lot of catching up to do. Only when the world had been put to rights to the satisfaction of both, did Blotto return to the main house.

On entering the hall, he was buttonholed by his sister, who instantly whisked him away to her boudoir.

Once there, Twinks started on another kind of Jaw, rather more animated than the one she had just delivered at Perylgrim. She recommended to Blotto a state of extreme vigilance. She pointed out to him – facts he had forgotten – that, as well as being accused of two murders, he had added to his charge-sheet the offence of escaping from one of His Majesty's Prisons. It was more than likely that the police would want to recapture him and make him face trial for these misdemeanours.

Twinks advised her brother to be cautious and not to

venture too far outside Tawcester Towers itself. The ancestral pile contained enough rooms for him to lie low in and escape detection for a considerable time. In the surrounding estate he would be more visible and vulnerable to re-arrest.

Blotto gave a good impression of someone who was taking his sister's advice seriously, though he had no intention of following it. He would continue to wander round the family domain at will. The drive from main road to mansion was over a mile. The porter in the lodge at the gates would alert him to any suspicious police activity.

Twinks didn't mention to her brother that the following day, the Friday, would see the arrival at Tawcester Towers of Sir Albert Anstruther, who had been invited for the Aristotours weekend. The Chief Constable of Tawcestershire's re-encounter with his escaped murder suspect was a problem they would deal with when it arose.

She then showed her brother the Aristotours invitation.

He read it with mounting horror. 'Toad-in-the-hole!' he said. 'The ghastible stenchers! That's way the wrong side of wrong!'

'You're bong on the nose there, Blotters!'

'To offer hunting when the cricket season hasn't even ended! I've never before come across sponge-worms as oikish as this! And to have the brazen crust to call people like us "The Other Half"! That's horraciously insulting! We're a much smaller fraction than that!'

'Less than one spoffing per cent,' said Twinks, who knew about such things.

'Fair biddles,' said Blotto. 'Though I've never really understood decimation.'

'Decimals,' his sister corrected gently.

'Tickey-tockey. Anyway, the boddoes to whom this invitation will appeal are not the kind of slugbuckets we want in Tawcester Towers!'

'You've pinged the partridge there, Blotters. And you haven't yet had a chance to see the other murdy changes these Aristotours out-of-bounders are making to the ancestral pile.'

'What have the four-faced filchers done?'

'They've redecorated the guest bedrooms and put on new mattresses and bedding.'

'New sheets?'

'New sheets,' his sister confirmed.

'Not damp ones?'

'Not damp ones.'

'Broken biscuits!' said Blotto. He only used such extreme language when he was deeply upset. And there was nothing more likely to upset him than the ending of the fine tradition, which had lasted down the centuries, of beds in English stately homes having damp sheets.

'Is there nothing we can do,' he asked pitifully, 'to stop this desiccation?'

'I think the word you're looking for,' suggested Twinks gently, 'is "desecration".'

'That too,' said Blotto. 'But is there no way we can stop this weekend being taken over by accountants, solicitors and similar slugbuckets?'

'Well, I was given a thoughtette on a possible solution,' said Twinks, 'and from a very unlikely source . . .'

She proceeded to tell Blotto the idea that Rodney Perkins had put forward in the Tawcester Towers cellar.

'So . . .' said Blotto, piecing things together slowly, as was his wont, 'for every genuine article we can get along here to join the gorging and gulping, that's another oikish sponge-worm off the dance card?'

'*Exactamento*,' said Twinks.

'Then why in the name of strawberries haven't you asked Loofah to get his House of Lords bush telegraph going?'

'Ah. I had that thought, Blotto me old horseshoe nail-puller, but Loofah didn't want to play snap.'

'Why not, by Denzil?'

'I think the Mater had got him in crimps.'

Blotto nodded. That would explain it.

'Anyway,' Twinks continued disconsolately, 'even if she hadn't, I don't know whether the H of L bush telegraph would have got moving quick enough ... unless there was some really powerful incentive to get them to pongle over to T.T.'

'Yes, time may be playing for the opposition now, Twinks me old leather insole,' said Blotto.

But he wasn't as defeated as he sounded. In the echoing spaces of his cranium, an embryonic idea was pushing against the walls of its shell. A real buzzbanger of an idea. People wrote off Blotto at their peril. Maybe he had thought of a way to bring the cream of English aristocracy to Tawcester Towers for the 'How The Other Half Live' weekend ...?

On the Friday morning, Twinks's personal maid summoned her mistress from her boudoir to take a telephone call.

It came from Professor Erasmus Holofernes, whose academic assiduity had been replaced by something approaching panic. 'My dear young woman,' he said as soon as she came on the line, 'I have had some disturbing news about the Secret Congregation of the Crooked Hand.'

'What diddler's hand have the SCOTCH stenchers been playing this time?' asked Twinks.

'That's what's worrying,' replied the Professor. 'I don't know exactly what they're up to, but some major atrocity is being planned, something that will destroy part of the fabric of British society.'

'Do you know where it's happening? Or the names of any of the slugbuckets involved?'

'Sadly, no. The information I have is not strong on detail, but I'm certain it's true in outline. The news comes from reliable sources.'

'Hm,' said Twinks. 'And are you any closer to establishing the link between SCOTCH and the Aristotours lumps of toadspawn?'

'Again, frustratingly, no. I'm sure there is a link, though. And I'm sure Baron Chipping Norton is involved.'

'Wouldn't knock my hat off to find he was,' said Twinks. 'He's as devious as a three-dollar note.'

'Hm. And he's going to be at this Aristotours weekend you've got coming up at Tawcester Towers, is he?'

'Sure as a gold sovereign he'll be here.'

'Well, be very careful, Twinks. The information I've received suggests that the Crooked Hand will actually be overseeing the atrocity himself.'

'You aren't dabbing the digit at Baron Chipping Norton as the Crooked Hand, are you?'

'I don't think so. I wish I could tell you more.' The Professor sounded deeply distressed. 'All I can say is, Twinks, this weekend . . . be very careful.'

Blotto and Twinks's earlier visit to the Duke of Tawcester in the East Wing had been a rarity, but for Blotto to seek out his brother on his own was rarer still. As Twinks had done, he found Loofah sitting at his desk looking out of the window.

'Afternoon, bro,' said Blotto.

'Afternoon,' the Duke reciprocated.

'All tickey-tockey?'

'Erm . . . Well . . . Fact is, Sloggo's pregnant again.'

'Good ticket! You've won the coconut!'

'It'll be another girl,' said Loofah morosely.

The likelihood was so strong that Blotto didn't offer any counter-argument. Instead, he went on, 'The mutual sis said you weren't planning to invite any of the peerage to this weekend's jim-jamboree . . . ?'

'The mutual sis was right.'

'Though you know that every boddo of the right sort picking up the invite means there'll be space for one less oikish sponge-worm . . . ?'

The Duke of Tawcester shrugged and just said two words. 'The Mater . . .'

That confirmed Blotto's suspicion that the case was unarguable. So, he moved on with his new plan. 'Did you know, Loofah,' he asked casually, 'that Lady Cynthia Westbury has just broken off her engagement to the son of the Earl of Frinton?'

'No, I didn't,' said the Duke. Which was hardly surprising, because Blotto had just made up both names.

'Well, this means,' said Blotto, elaborating further, 'that the plumpilicious Cynthia is back on the marriage market and available at cat's meat prices.'

'What has that to do with me, Blotto?' asked his brother, with the weariness of a married man facing yet another pregnancy,

'The plumpilicious Cynthia's mother is American, bred amongst oil wells, so there's lots of the old jingle-jangle.'

'Are you proposing to make a bid for her yourself, Blotto?'

'Not in a donkey's lifetime, Loofah. I'm a younger son, apart from anything else, and Cynthia's a definite title-truffler. But I have a friend from my Club . . .'

'That's the Gren?'

'Old Grenadiers, that's the Johnny. Anyway, my friend's called Lolly. Heir to the Duke of Mevagissy, and he's currently finding things a little tight in the trousering department – lack of spondulicks, you know.' Two more joined Blotto's list of fictional characters. His imagination was working overtime.

'Then why don't you alert him to the sudden availability of this golden gravy-boat Cynthia?'

'Because, dear bro of mine, I've lost the boddo's telephone number.'

'Well, I don't have it.'

'I didn't think you'd have it, Loofah, but I thought you might still have the membership lists for the Heirs Apparent.'

'Ah, Blotto. On the same page now. The fact is, I do still have the lists.'

The Heirs Apparent was a kind of informal club, a freemasonry of young men who were heirs to aristocratic titles. The association proved useful for checking out how much closer to disinheritance someone's bad behaviour had brought them, whose gambling debts exceeded the property they stood to inherit and, as in Blotto's fictional scenario, what wealthy young heiresses had just become available.

Reaching into the drawer of his desk, the Duke of Tawcester produced the list, handed it over to his brother and was, as ever, vastly relieved to see the back of him.

Blotto had not, in the past, made many telephone calls. Though the apparatus was useful for firming up arrangements, he did not regard it as a medium for conversation. Still, he massively increased his telephone-calling average that evening.

Never before had the Tawsworthy operator had to connect calls with so many butlers.

But at the end, requiring Grimshaw to supply him with continuous brandies and soda in the billiard room, an exhausted Blotto felt extremely pleased with his evening's work.

The next day, Mr Weissfeder, the Tawcester Towers Master of the Revels, felt considerably less pleased to be constantly summoned to the telephone. Each call followed the same pattern. Another Heir Apparent wished to participate in the 'How The Other Half Live' weekend.

And each of those calls was followed by another, in which Mr Weissfeder had to stand down – and refund the payment of – an accountant or solicitor, for whom there would no longer be room at the event.

Blotto felt more than pleased – he felt ecstatic that his plan had worked.

And he did mentally acknowledge Loofah's contribution to its success. He reminded himself of the old proverb that two heads were better than one, conveniently forgetting that it was predicated on the intellectual quality of the two heads in question.

Huh, thought Blotto, there were people – like his sister Twinks, it had to be said – who didn't think he could plan his way out of a one-bush maze. He'd show them.

23

More Suspicious Guests

The programme of events for the 'How The Other Half Live' weekend at Tawcester Towers more or less followed the pattern of the one at Clusters. The guests would arrive late Friday afternoon, there would be a major dinner in the Great Hall on the Saturday night, followed by a séance with Signora Zucchini. And the rest of the time the paying oikish sponge-worms would be allowed to mingle with The Other Half and find out How They Lived. That was the plan.

Except of course, as it turned out – thanks to the success of Blotto's fiendish scheme – there were no oikish sponge-worms. The guests all belonged to The Other Half ... or that much tinier fraction which represented the British aristocracy. And mingling with each other wasn't that much of a novelty.

Though Tawcester Towers's Master of the Revels, Mr Weissfeder, was in charge on the ground, Baron Chipping Norton was also present, keeping a watching brief over the event. And he was having an extremely uncomfortable time. Not only had the take-up of places by genuine aristocrats removed any possibility of Aristotours making any profit from the weekend, their presence also made him acutely aware of his own inferior status. Peers who were the genuine article did not demonstrate much in the way of empathy for *parvenus* who had bought their titles in a Lloyd George clearance sale.

The Baron was generally ignored and, if he did manage to get into conversation with any of the guests, patronised and soon frozen out.

The assembled scions of noble houses did not particularly care about the weekend's entertainments, as offered by Aristotours, either. They could get all that at their own stately homes. What did interest them was the announcement that Blotto's phone call had promised would be made after the séance on the Saturday night.

Twinks had decided it would be sensible to keep her brother out of the public eye on the Friday evening. Which, when she was confronted by an extremely aerated Chief Constable of Tawcestershire, proved to be a wise precaution.

'So, what have you to say for yourself?' he demanded.

'Good evening, Sir Albert,' she replied coolly. 'Splendissimo to see you.' A little, puzzled smile. 'Why, what else did you expect me to say for myself?'

'I know what you were doing on Thursday evening at Perylgrim!'

'So do I. I was actually present in the clinkbox at the time, so my recollection of the occasion is perfect. I was giving a Jaw to the Prison Governor and his staff on the subject of General Sir Hudson Lowe.'

'But that wasn't all you were doing!'

'You're bong on the nose there, Sir Albert. As an accompaniment to my Jaw, I was showing lantern slides. And if you wish me to do a repeat performance for other members of the Tawcestershire Constabulary, I would love it as a pike loves troutlings. I'm sure it would be of particular benefit to some of your boddoes in the prison service to learn about the achievements of General Sir Hudson Lowe.'

'Lady Honoria,' said the Chief Constable, almost stamping his foot in frustration, 'you know that while you were giving your lecture there, your brother escaped from Perylgrim!'

'Did he?' Twinks asked innocently. 'Well, that's a coincidence. While little *moi* was actually on the prems?'

'I demand you tell me the current location of Lord Devereux Lyminster!'

Never has so much innocence been seen in azure eyes as the ones Twinks turned on the Chief Constable. 'Are you sure he isn't still in your clinkbox? Have you looked in all the corners?'

Rather than a deprivation, Blotto regarded his exclusion from the festivities a huge bonus. Though he'd been appalled at the prospect of mixing with oikish spongeworms like accountants and solicitors, mixing with his own sort was not a very appealing prospect either. He knew they'd only drink too much and bray at him. Which would make him drink too much and bray back at them.

Also, there was the serious risk that he might, tongue loosened by alcohol, let slip to one of them the falsity of the subterfuge by which he had brought them to Tawcester Towers that weekend.

Fortunately, he knew the perfect hideaway for such situations. Above Mephistopheles's stall. In the stable block, there was a hayloft which had been provided with the basic accoutrements of a bedroom. He'd once asked Corky Froggett why the facility was there, and never thought to question the chauffeur's reply that the space could accommodate a groom if one of the horses was sick or about to deliver a foal.

Anyway, whatever its usual function, for Blotto it offered the perfect bolthole.

That Friday evening, he organised Corky to bring him a tray of covered dishes from the kitchens. This was an area where the efforts of Mr Ulrich Weissfeder had had a beneficial effect. The meal Blotto enjoyed in the hayloft, identical to that served to the guests in the Great Hall, was a significant step up from the customary nursery food produced by the Tawcester Towers kitchens.

Mr Weissfeder had also had some influence over the wines being served that evening. Supplies in the cellar of the stately home had been running low, and the remaining bottles were more distinctive for the number of cobwebs enfolding them than their quality. The Master of the Revels had supplied much better wines from the Aristotours cellars.

Corky Froggett brought to the hayloft two bottles of an excellent 1903 Château Margaux. And a third, in case the young master felt thirsty. Which, inevitably, he did.

So Blotto had a blissful evening in his eyrie above the stall, wherein lived one of the three loves of his life. As night took over, the snuffling from Mephistopheles melded in perfect harmony with the gentle snoring of his master.

They certainly slept better than the guests, for whom the Aristotours weekend had been originally planned, would have done.

Had the family and staff at Tawcester Towers been paying more attention, they might have questioned why Rodney Perkins's army of workmen had been installing as much electrical wiring throughout the house as they had plumbers' piping. Though the massive boiler might require mains power, the individual radiators did not need electricity. The hot water should just flow through the closed system, impelled by the boiler's pump.

Twinks, of all people, should have been aware of the anomaly, particularly since she had actually been down to the cellar to see Rodney Perkins. But his brilliant idea for excluding oikish sponge-worms from the weekend had taken all other thoughts from her mind and clouded her normally acute powers of observation.

She quickly pieced together what was happening, however, at the end of the Friday evening, when she was in her boudoir preparing for bed. The dinner she had just finished, though the food was excellent, had not been otherwise stimulating. Granted, she'd been spared the attentions of gawping accountants and solicitors trying to find out 'How The Other Half Lived'. But, as Blotto had anticipated, the company of her peers had left a great deal to be desired.

Her expectations had not been high. She had spent much time with scions of aristocratic family trees – indeed, many of the Heirs Apparent had at some point presented themselves as amorous swains in search of her hand in marriage. The daughter of a Duke was always a desirable chattel, and when that daughter came as perfectly packaged as Lady Honoria Lyminster . . . well, the competition was as fierce as the British aristocracy had seen since the Wars of the Roses.

But, in spite of the fact that Twinks had very firmly slapped down all of the scions with dynastic ambitions for her, that Friday evening it seemed that none of them had taken her discouragement to heart. She was treated to far too many glances of admiration from goggle-eyes, and sly smiles from lips unsupported by chins. All the Heirs Apparent seemed to believe that, yes, they may have failed in their previous endeavours, but now they were starting again with a clean slate. And this time they were in with a good chance of snaring her as a bride. It was, for Twinks, a most unnerving experience.

Which was why she was so relieved finally to be alone in her boudoir, making plans for the rest of the weekend. Scattered over her dressing table were a large number of financial newspapers and magazines. Some of these she had collected herself, others had been sent from Oxford by Professor Erasmus Holofernes.

She started going through the documentation, tracing the price fluctuations of certain shares. It didn't take her long to find some interesting anomalies. Anomalies which even the most charitable of observers would have recognised as actionable.

Satisfied by that result, she then focused her supercharged mind on her main ambition for the weekend, to prove, once and for all, the connection between Aristotours and the Secret Congregation of the Crooked Hand. Knowing about the false dossiers which had been created to incriminate her brother, Twinks was determined to provide one herself that would finger the real criminals.

From her sequinned reticule, she withdrew a silver-covered notebook and a silver propelling pencil. She then, to clarify the details in her mighty mind, wrote notes about the various scenarios which might potentially develop over the next couple of days.

Just after one in the morning, still busy in her boudoir, Twinks heard the first of the sounds.

It began with a clanking, heavy, metallic booming through the corridors of the old house. Her first thought was that it must be something to do with the new heating system whose installation Rodney Perkins had just completed.

But while heating systems are adept at clanking, few of them moan and groan like souls in torment. And that was the next sound that invaded Tawcester Towers. Taken in context with the moaning, Twinks now identified the earlier metallic noises as the rattling of chains. Yes, there were ghosts about. Or someone wanted people to think there were ghosts about.

Lest there should be any doubt about this, the clanking and moaning were now joined by a sepulchral, echoing voice.

'I am the ghost,' it cried, 'of Rupert, Duke of Tawcester.'

167

'For the love of strawberries, narrow it down a bit!' said Twinks, out loud. 'Every spoffing Duke of Tawcester's called Rupert.'

As if hearing her – though of course it couldn't – the ghostly voice continued, 'I was known during my lifetime as Rupert the Cavalier . . .'

'Oh yes?' said Twinks sceptically. 'And I'm an Apache dancer.'

'. . . and I am doomed forever to walk the corridors of Tawcester Towers, shut out from heaven for a terrible crime that I committed.'

'What a load of globbins!' said Twinks, rising from her dressing table and issuing out into the corridor towards the source of this nonsense.

Meanwhile, the voice continued, 'To my eternal shame, I took advantage of a young woman, an innocent child from the town of Tawsworthy. I seduced her and then, when she fell pregnant, I abandoned her to poverty and ignominy. Before the birth of my bastard child, she drowned herself in the River Taw. And for this crime, I am doomed forever to drag my chains along these corridors and terrify the guests at Tawcester Towers!'

While this litany of shame went on, Twinks searched along the panelled walls for its source. She knew what she was looking for and berated herself for her inadequate observational skills. She should have taken notice earlier of the electrical wiring being laid around the house and recognised its function.

Ah . . . She'd found it. The wires had been hidden behind the panelling. The loudspeaker itself was attached to the back of a family portrait. And, as she approached, Twinks not only understood how the ghostly narrative had been achieved, she also recognised, through the echo and chain-rattling, the voice of the impersonator.

What's more, she noticed that the hidden electrical device wasn't just a speaker. It had a two-way function. Not only could ghostly emanations be broadcast from, presumably, the cellar. Communication could also be made from this corridor – and doubtless others throughout Tawcester Towers – back to the speaker down below.

Twinks waited until the false Rupert the Cavalier finished his confession and indulged in a little more gratuitous chain-rattling and moaning, before she approached the device, pressed down its speaker button and said, very firmly, 'I would like you to know, Baron Chipping Norton, that your slanderous attack on the integrity of the Lyminster family is achieving nothing.

'What is more, in your attempt to blacken the reputation of my ancestors, you have got your spoffing facts completely wrong about the Duke who seduced a girl from Tawsworthy and caused her to commit suicide by drowning in the River Taw. Anyone who wasn't an ignorant slugbucket would know that it wasn't Rupert the Cavalier who ruined that poor girl.

'It was Rupert the Fiend!'

Twinks's intervention put an end to further visitations that night. The only point of having ghostly ancestors clanking along the corridors of Tawcester Towers was to inspire terror. Baron Chipping Norton and whoever else he was working with down in the cellar pretty soon realised that they weren't achieving that desired result.

The whole elaborate illusion had been created for the guests who had originally been expected. A Tawcester Towers full of oikish sponge-worms like accountants and solicitors, together with their hysterical wives, would have been properly frightened and thrilled by the manifestation of Rupert the Cavalier and his guilty conscience.

They would have felt they were getting their money's worth for their 'How The Other Half Live' weekend. Haunting had been one of the amenities they had expected from the event and would have provided much conversation around their dinner tables (or wherever people of that sort ate their meals). They would have enjoyed the *frisson* of fear.

But, for the clientele who did actually occupy the guest bedrooms of Tawcester Towers that night, the paranormal offered very little. They all had much more convincing family ghosts in their own stately homes.

Few of the bedded-down Heirs Apparent were even aware of Rupert the Cavalier's caterwauling. And those who were wakened by it, very quickly turned over in their beds and went back to sleep.

24

Twinks Prepares

Twinks woke on the Saturday morning feeling disconsolate. The customary 'Sunny' setting of her emotional barometer was moving in the direction of 'Changeable'. Partly, she hadn't had her normal ration of beauty sleep (in her case a literal expression – mind you, she was equally beautiful when awake). She also didn't relish running the gauntlet of more noble scions who suddenly were under the illusion that they stood a chance with her.

But there was another, deeper, reason for her disquiet. The setting-up of the elaborate speaker system, along with the bedroom refurbishment overseen by Ulrich Weissfeder, suggested again that Aristotours had a long-term agenda for Tawcester Towers.

Not for the first time, Twinks worried about the kind of agreement that her mother might have signed with Aristotours.

Blotto woke to no barometric troubles. As ever, set fair to 'Sunny'.

And Corky Froggett had come up with the silverware so far as breakfast was concerned. A comprehensive raid on the chafing dishes had produced even more than the young master's usual healthy ration of rashers and so on.

All this, and Mephistopheles on hand to chew over the fat with. Blotto, who had forgotten he was still charged with two murders and an escape from His Majesty's Prison of Perylgrim, thought everything was creamy éclair. He was definitely rolling on camomile lawns.

He even wondered about not going back to his bedroom in Tawcester Towers and spending the rest of his nights in the hayloft. For ever.

Back in the great house, there was not a lot of activity. The Heirs Apparent, well fed and watered the night before, were not early risers. Most of them tended to hit the chafing dishes some time after eleven.

And none wanted to participate in any of the guided tours and other activities laid on for the weekend's original guests. They didn't need to know 'How The Other Half Lived'. They could get all that at home.

Twinks sought out Grimshaw in his pantry. To any casual observer, the butler would have looked as impassive as ever. Twinks, knowing him well, could detect from the tiniest change of angle of his chin that he was deeply distressed.

'What's put lumps in your custard, Grimshaw me old bottle-brush?' she asked cheerily.

'Nothing, milady. According to long-established custom, everything at Tawcester Towers is exactly as it should be.'

Though she knew he was not telling the truth, she did not argue. She respected his determination to do his job, whatever the circumstances.

'Just had a thoughtette, Grimshaw . . .'

'Yes, milady?'

'Want to truffle out some gin-gen on one of the guests. Could you show me the bedroom batting order?'

'Of course, milady.'

He produced a typewritten sheet, headed: 'ARISTO-TOURS GUEST LIST'. Seeing his aristocratic superior raising a perfect eyebrow, he couldn't help saying, with an edge of bitterness, 'They were gracious enough to vouchsafe me a copy.'

Twinks made no comment, just checked which bedroom was being occupied by the person she was interested in.

'Talking of Aristotours, Grimshaw,' she said, 'I've been looking for that stencher Baron Chipping Norton. Haven't clapped your peepers on him recently, have you?'

'I have indeed, milady. I believe you will find him in the Brown Withdrawing Room.'

'What, in the name of snitchrags, is he doing there?'

'I think Your Ladyship would be well advised to put that question to the Baron himself,' replied Grimshaw, betraying his intense emotion only by the briefest flicker of a left eyebrow.

The Brown Withdrawing Room was situated adjacent to the butler's pantry and, before she even entered it, Twinks could see the cause of Grimshaw's disquiet. On the oak-panelled door had been fixed a name-plate (not even made of brass) which read: 'ARISTOTOURS OFFICE'.

To Twinks, this was an act of outright hogcheek. Ever since the appointment of Ulrich Weissfeder as Master of the Revels, it had been clear that Aristotours wanted to supplant the management of Tawcester Towers, but up until this point they had employed a level of subtlety. Commandeering one of the great house's principal rooms as an office was going way beyond the barbed wire.

Once again, Twinks questioned the level of her mother's involvement in the takeover. The whole set-up had the Dowager Duchess's dabs all over it. And Twinks had no doubt that all of the maternal diktats had been rubber-stamped by her son, Rupert the Insipid.

173

Deliberately making as much noise as she could, Twinks flung open the door of the Brown Withdrawing Room.

Two pairs of eyes looked up from the desk where they had been perusing papers. They belonged to Baron Chipping Norton and Ulrich Weissfeder. Both pairs looked guilty.

The Baron was first to replace the guilt with something bland and mildly seductive. As ever, he was aware of his stature and good looks. 'Lady Honoria, it is, as ever, an enormous pleasure to see you.'

She was in no mood to reciprocate the sentiment. 'Next time you try to impersonate our spoffing ancestors,' she said, 'do try to be up to mustard with the factettes!'

He looked pleasingly discomfited. The ear-blasting he'd received the night before from the speaker in the cellar had made its mark.

'A lot of jingle-jangle it must have set you back,' she said, 'to set up all that electrical gubbins for the one peasly little night. Particularly since you've completely got the wrong end of the sink plunger with regard to the guests. Accountants, solicitors and other debased life-forms may be impressed by leadpenny hauntings. You won't get a flickerette of interest from the genuine article. As you saw. So snubbins to you – what?'

'So far as Aristotours is concerned,' said the Baron smoothly, 'last night was a particularly useful rehearsal, which proved to us that all of our electrical apparatus works.'

'Well, give that pony a rosette!' said Twinks sarcastically. 'What a pity that, after the one solitary night, you will have to remove all your electrical apparatus and scuttle it down the River of No Return!'

That produced a thin smile from the Baron. 'I regret to inform you, Lady Honoria, that we will be doing no such thing. All of the improvements Aristotours have made to Tawcester Towers have been sanctioned and approved by your brother the Duke. So, I'm afraid there is nothing you can do about any of it.'

'Don't you believe it, Baron! The blood of the Lyminsters may have dried to a trickle in Loofah's veins, but it's throbbing like Peggy Riley in Blotto's and mine. You won't—'

'Oh, talking of your brother Blotto,' Baron Chipping Norton intervened, 'I thought you'd like to know that the Chief Constable, Sir Albert Anstruther, is here and—'

'I saw the poor pineapple last night and had a chatette with him.'

'Well, Lady Honoria, you may take the murder charges against your brother lightly. I can assure you he doesn't.'

'He did gab on a bit about that, yes.'

'He's more than gabbing now. He's called out the full manpower of the Tawcestershire Constabulary to search the estate. He's convinced that your precious Blotto is still here somewhere.'

'What makes him convinced of that?'

'The Chief Constable said – and I quote – "Lord Devereux Lyminster wouldn't have the imagination to hide anywhere else."'

Twinks was about to argue on behalf of her brother when she realised that, of course, Bertie Anstruther was right.

'There was another person,' said Ulrich Weissfeder in his precise Swiss accent, 'who was looking for your brother.'

'Oh?'

'One of the guests. The Earl of Cleckheaton. It seems that at school he and your brother toasted puffins together.'

'That would be "muffins",' said Twinks.

'Ah. Well, he wished your brother to organise something for tomorrow.'

'So, maybe,' said Baron Chipping Norton with a supercilious smile, 'you could tell Blotto that when you see him . . . unless, of course, the Chief Constable has already made the re-arrest.'

* * *

The next part of Twinks's preparation for the evening ahead took her through the corridors which linked the Tawcester Towers kitchens to the Great Hall. There she found exactly what she had expected to find. The stepladder was a folding one, prevented from doing the splits when opened by a restraining rope attached to the sides.

Twinks reached into her sequinned reticule and brought out a small but sharp pair of scissors.

'Toad-in-the-hole!' said Blotto enthusiastically. 'That would be pure creamy éclair!'

They were in the hayloft. Twinks had just told her brother of the Earl of Cleckheaton's hopes for the following day.

'Cleckers was one of my major chumboes at Eton. We got up to all kinds of rags together. Remember we were once having an ink fight, using spoffing rulers to flick soaked blotch bombs at each other, and one of the beaks came through the door and an ink bomb caught him bong on the conk . . .' He collapsed in laughter at the recollection.

'And if Cleckers wants me to roust up a cricket match for tomorrow . . . well, I'd be as happy as a duck in orange!'

'Rein in the roans for a moment there,' said Twinks. 'Bertie Anstruther is here on the prems and he's determined to re-arrest you for the two murders you're accused of.'

'Tickey-tockey, sister of mine. But don't forget, last time there was something as important as a cricket match at stake – the little frolic against the Marquis of Hartlepool's Irrelevancies – he let me burst like a butterfly from Tawsworthy police station to wield the willow. I'm sure he'd serve up the same sausages if he knew the match'd be against Cleckers.'

'I wouldn't put my last laddered silk stocking on it, Blotters. Bertie Anstruther's blue touchpaper is now extremely close to the flame and—'

'Milord! Young master!' She was interrupted by a red-faced Corky Froggett, rushing up the ladder from Mephistopheles's stable.

'The rozzers are on their way!' the chauffeur shouted. 'Look!' And he pointed out of the hayloft's small window to the drive from the main gates. Along it proceeded a convoy of police cars, with a Black Maria bringing up the rear.

'They are coming to arrest you, milord!'

'Don't don your worry-boots, Corky! I've got my cricket bat with me . . . ' Blotto produced it from under the hay '. . . and these are the kind of odds a Lyminster fancies!'

Twinks could have predicted that would be her brother's reaction, but her approach was more practical. 'Is there a way of getting him out of this horracious gluepot, Corky?'

'There is, milady,' said the chauffeur, almost smugly. 'Follow me!'

He led them down into Mephistopheles's stable. Blotto had to be discouraged from getting too deep into conversation with his hunter, as Corky Froggett shifted some bales of hay to reveal the opening of a trapdoor. He grabbed the recessed metal ring and lifted the hatch. 'Down there, milord! You'll be fine.'

'Tickey-tockey,' said Blotto, gripping his cricket bat and making his way into the darkness.

Mephistopheles whinnied a farewell to his disappearing master.

With the trapdoor closed and the hay bales replaced, Twinks grinned at the chauffeur. 'You've won the coconut, Corky! I thought I knew every speck of dust at Tawcester Towers, but I've never clapped the old peepers on that. How do you come to know about it?'

'Came upon the trapdoor by chance one day when I was tidying up.'

'And I'll bet a guinea to a groat you've found it useful sometimes.'

'Everything is useful on the right occasion,' said Corky Froggett judiciously.

But he avoided the young mistress's eye. He knew that she knew how useful he had found the secret tunnel for spiriting kitchen maids away from the big house to the stable area. Where there were not only nice, soft, welcoming bales of hay but also a nice, soft, welcoming bed.

Chief Inspector Trumbull and Sergeant Knatchbull had been delegated by their Chief Constable to search the garage and stable blocks. These stood adjacent and, only a decade earlier, before the widespread development of the internal combustion engine, had all been stables.

By the time Tawcestershire Constabulary's finest arrived, Twinks had returned to the main house and Corky Froggett was lovingly giving the young master's Lagonda a bonus polish.

'We have to search everything,' announced Trumbull. 'We're on the trail of a double murderer.'

'Of course, Chief Inspector,' said Corky obsequiously. He gestured round the garage area. 'Be my guest.'

After a detailed search, Trumbull said, 'We need to look inside the car.'

'Of course, Chief Inspector.' Helpfully, the chauffeur unlocked the Lagonda.

Another fruitless search concluded, a new look of cunning came into Trumbull's eye. 'And we need to check the dickey too.'

Corky Froggett didn't think it the moment to mention that, after some bodywork alterations performed by the Chicago Mafia, the Lagonda had, beneath the chassis, a secret compartment with space for two fugitives – or two corpses, come to that. Instead, he moved to the back of the car and opened the dickey. Again, nothing untoward was revealed.

'Now the weather's got better, Chief Inspector,' Corky

could not refrain from observing, 'I bet you're really appreciating your sunroof at Tawsworthy police station.'

Both Trumble and Knatchbull gave him looks of deep suspicion, but neither pursued the subject. Their expressions returned to the factory setting of 'Baffled'.

'Stables next,' said Trumbull, extra loudly to show his authority.

Corky did not follow them through. He just listened to Mephistopheles's whinnied anger at having two strangers in his domain.

Chief Inspector Trumbull and Sergeant Knatchbull inspected every square inch of the stable block, even dragging their over-indulged bodies by ladder up to the haylofts. The only space they hadn't explored was Mephistopheles's stall.

The two policemen looked at each other nervously. Annoyed by the fact that the intruders were still there, the hunter flared his mighty nostrils and hurled himself against the door of his stall, kicking his heavy shoes against the splintering wood.

Trumbull and Knatchbull made good their escape to Tawcester Towers.

Once the trapdoor had slammed shut over his head, Blotto found himself in a maze of tunnels. They were not very deep. Ground-level grilles at the top of the walls allowed in enough light for him to see his way.

He had taken on board the potential danger of the police search and, for once, judged that this was not the moment for quixotic gestures. In terms of derring-do, that was a derring-don't.

So, he decided to wait until the search had been called off. Finding a comfortable niche, commanding a view, through a slit in the stone, of the main drive, he settled in. He would move back into the main body of Tawcester Towers once the police convoy had left.

Full of the large breakfast Corky had brought him, not to mention the large lunch and accompanying wines, Blotto, innocent as a baby, clutching his cricket bat, was soon asleep.

Twinks did not put a lot of effort into dressing for that evening's dinner. But, some half an hour before the pre-prandial drinks (with accompanying jazz band – the Aristotours formula did not change), she slipped along the corridors towards the bedroom whose resident's name she had checked out on the list in Grimshaw's pantry.

And she put her considerable powers of persuasion to the test.

25

Unhappy Medium

The Heirs Apparent hadn't been interested in the family ghosts because they all had their own supply of those, but the idea of a séance did tickle their aristocratic fancies. As a class, they had not been encouraged to communicate with their parents – and indeed had rarely seen them – so, after that generation passed away, there were a lot of basic questions that needed asking. Questions like where various keys had been left, whether the original documentation of shareholdings had been filed, what was written on the birth certificates of family members who'd been conceived the wrong side of the blanket ... So, there were practical reasons for wanting to make contact with the Other Side.

Also, the event might be a laugh. And the scions of the noble houses of England really enjoyed a laugh. Particularly when they had just been gorging and gulping the finest food Ulrich Weissfeder could extract from the Tawcester Towers kitchens and the finest wines the Aristo-tours cellar could provide.

One striking difference from the previous séance at Clusters was that, in the Great Hall that night, there were no women. The Heirs Apparent to whom Blotto had extended the invitation to the weekend at Tawcester Towers were all unmarried. The Dowager Duchess, shrewdly, kept well clear of the whole circus. Sloggo was unwell, her latest morning sickness now stretching right through the day. And, after dinner, Twinks too seemed to have made her escape.

So, there was a raucous masculine level of anticipation in the Great Hall before Signora Zucchini started to work her magic.

'I am extremely sensitive to the aura of buildings,' that heavily accented, high, birdlike voice trilled once again.

She then went through the same litany about the ancient stones that created Tawcester Towers being the repositories of history and the dead wishing to speak through her. With appropriate shivering and spasms, she could once again hear 'voices, many, many voices.' And she asked the throng of Heirs Apparent whether they wanted to hear those voices.

The well-clareted unchinned in the audience bellowed a positive response.

But, with her next words, she stilled them. 'I demand,' she said, 'complete silence from you all while I make contact with the Other Side.'

The tiny, black-clad body went through its routine of twitches. The arms once again did their anchored seaweed impression, before her spine seemed to buckle and her limbs drooped as if insensate.

When she next spoke, Signora Zucchini's voice had changed completely. From the mouth which so recently piped an Italian accent, came the sound of a strong man, born to privilege ... not unlike many of the Heirs Apparent in the Great Hall.

And a flickering light outlined the portrait of Rupert the Cavalier, high on the wall behind her. 'Welcome to Tawcester Towers,' he boomed. He followed that with a welcome to the Other Side. And for both sentences, his lips appeared to move in time with the speech.

Then there was a reference to – and apology for – the

haunting that the deceased Duke had inflicted on the house guests the previous night. Since they had all slept through it, this didn't mean a lot to the Heirs Apparent. But Signora Zucchini's script had not been amended to reflect the change of circumstances. After all, the weekend had now just become a rehearsal for the next event, when all the guests would be oikish sponge-worms, who paid for their entertainment.

Moving on, Rupert the Cavalier next assured his audience that he was willing to answer any questions with which they might challenge the wisdom of the dead, gathered in readiness on the Other Side.

The next little scene was an exact repeat of what had happened at Clusters. Someone, clearly an Aristotours plant, went through the rigmarole of wanting to contact his recently deceased butler. They hadn't even bothered to change the name from Hargreaves. Again, the poor man had died smashing his employer's Hispano-Suiza into a tree.

And yes, the pay-off was the questioner asking the whereabouts of the key to the wine cellar. The reply, emanating from the tiny Signora Zucchini in a fruity butler voice, was still: 'On top of the cupboard in my pantry!'

This exchange so accurately reflected the concerns – and the sense-of-humour level – of the Heirs Apparent, that it was greeted by huge laughter.

Another Aristotours plant then put the question about financial expertise. Was there someone on the Other Side who could give advice on the current state of the British Stock Market?

The tiny figure in black, speaking in the voice of Rupert the Cavalier, assured the petitioner that the Other Side was bursting with financial experts who not only understood the past history of world finance but could also predict the future fate of any investment.

'Excellent!' said the questioner. 'Just the kind of chaps I need. So, will you ask them: should I sell my remaining

183

shares in British Amalgamated Screws? They had been outperforming many other stocks in recent months but things seem suddenly to have changed. What does your deceased investor say I should do? Cut my losses and sell the rest of the stock?'

'Absolutely not!' roared the late financial adviser being channelled by Rupert the Cavalier. 'Hang on to all you have and buy as many more as you can! The shares are currently at cat's meat prices. Not only will your actions in buying make you a fortune, they will also thwart the illegal manipulation of the Stock Market by investors from a company called Aristotours!'

This reply was greeted by silence, broken only by the sound of pencils scribbling notes on cuffs and dinner menus, to remind the Heirs Apparent to get on to their stockbrokers first thing on the Monday morning.

'What is more,' Rupert the Cavalier boomed on, 'if ever anyone advises you to buy shares in Aristotours themselves, avoid them like the plague! A dossier on their financial malpractices is soon to be presented to the City authorities. It is only a matter of time before all of Aristotours' directors will be in prison and the company liquidated!'

Shocked intakes of breath and more scribbling on paper were joined, just then, by another sound. Laughter. The Heirs Apparent had suddenly noticed that the lips of Rupert the Cavalier, which up until recently had moved in perfect synchronicity with the words emanating from Signora Zucchini, seemed to have lost the plot. The deceased Duke was frankly gibbering in silence.

Then, broadcast through the Great Hall, there was a crash, followed by a loud thump, a cry and an all-too-audible swear word. Someone well attuned to sound might have recognised this sequence as:

1. The noise of a sabotaged hinged stepladder collapsing,

2. The impact on the floor of the person falling from said stepladder,
3. The cry of pain from said person hitting the floor, and
4. The reaction of said person to his accident.

Twinks was a very honourable young woman. If she made a promise, she kept it. So, at the end of the séance, she went straight to the bedroom.

There, before removing the silken gag and releasing Signora Zucchini from the silk-covered but highly effective manacles, she divested herself of the medium's black costume and reassumed her own wardrobe. Then she put the gag and manacles back into her sequinned reticule.

As she had promised she would, she placed Signora Zucchini's script on the bedside table.

'I suggest,' she said kindly, 'that you cut all linkettes with this corrupt Aristotours set-up and pongle back to the theatre, where your skill with voices will be much better appreciated.'

'You know, I might and all,' said the small figure in broad Cockney. 'I've been thinking about doing something similar for a long time.'

'Good ticket,' said Twinks. 'May the luck of the Lyminsters go with you!'

Then, assuring the rather confused medium that everything in the future would be 'splendissimo' and 'pure creamy éclair', Twinks left the bedroom.

On the way back to her boudoir, she was stopped by a rather flustered Grimshaw. 'There is a telephone call for you, milady.'

Only one person would ring her at that time on a Saturday night. As soon as she picked up the apparatus, she said blithely, 'Hello, Razzy.'

'Twinks,' came the urgent response, 'you are in extreme danger! I have just received information as to the identity of the Crooked Hand. He is—'

The line cut out. Hardly surprising, given the fact that someone's hand had pressed down the telephone's cradle.

Twinks looked up into the unsmiling eyes of Baron Chipping Norton.

'Lady Honoria,' he said chillingly, 'I think it's time you came with me.'

26

Sedition in the Cellar

The Baron did not hold her as he led Twinks towards the cellar door. But he had his right hand in the pocket of his dinner jacket and she had no reason to disbelieve his assertion that there was a revolver at the end of it. The kind of slugbucket who'd frame her brother for two murders was capable of any kind of enormity.

While still on the ground floor, they passed a good number of the Heirs Apparent, but Twinks did not demean herself by asking them for help. She was a Lyminster, after all. They'd got through the Battle of Hastings, the Wars of the Roses, and the Civil War without asking help from anyone (except for thousands of expendable serfs). So now was not the moment to break that honourable tradition.

Besides, because of the lascivious way the claret- and brandy-filled scions of noble families greeted her as she passed, she didn't want to encourage them. Last thing she needed at that moment was some amorous swain casting her in the role of 'damsel in distress' and going into the full Galahad routine. That wouldn't help anyone.

No, as she had many times before, Twinks would test the depth of her current gluepot before devising the means to get out of it. Because get out of it she was sure she could.

No one observed Baron Chipping Norton open the door to the cellar and usher his captive through it.

There was a source of light at the far end of the cavernous space but, as soon as Twinks started down the brick steps into the void, she heard a heavy regular thrumming sound. She had been subconsciously aware of it in the body of the house, but there it had been drowned in the raucous badinage of the Heirs Apparent. Down in the cellar, it was loud and insistent.

With her extensive knowledge of engineering, Twinks identified the sound instantly. It was the newly installed heating system. The beast had been switched on and its oil power ignited. At that very moment, hot water was being pumped through the chain of radiators reaching into the furthest wings of Tawcester Towers. It was a remarkable technical achievement.

In other circumstances, Twinks would have sought out the person responsible – presumably Rodney Perkins – and slapped him on the back with a cheery 'Give that pony the Best of Show Rosette!'

But, somehow, with Baron Chipping Norton's hand now out of his pocket and the nose of his revolver making itself felt through the silk against her back, this didn't seem the moment.

As they approached the light source – and the boiler – Twinks saw that the master plumber was indeed present. What was more, the greetings exchanged by the two men showed they knew each other well. But their class difference was still maintained. Though Baron Chipping Norton's title had been bought at one of Lloyd George's basement sales, the plumber treated him as if he were the genuine article. Metaphorically, he still tugged the forelock that he didn't have.

Greetings exchanged, he asked, 'What can I do for you, milord?'

'This one . . .' The Baron dug his gun into Twinks's back for emphasis '. . . is proving rather troublesome.'

'In what way, milord?'

'She tried to sabotage the séance with Signora Zucchini.'

'Oh dear. How unfortunate.'

'In fact, she kidnapped and impersonated the genuine medium and—'

'Pardon my poke-in,' said Twinks, 'but I think what you mean when you say, "the genuine medium" is "the lead-penny thimble-jiggler who's been peddling a load of puddledash about—"'

She was silenced by a really painful jab from the revolver barrel.

'Anyway, Perkins,' the Baron went on, 'I think she needs to be cooled off down here for a while. I'll chain her to one of these uprights. Then I'll get some evidence made up that links her incontrovertibly to her brother's two murders. And we'll get the pair of them eliminated courtesy of His Majesty's gallows.'

'If you think anyone will believe a tissue-paper accusation against a member of the Lyminster family, then you're about as wrong as the man who thought he'd picked up a cooked prawn and put a live scorpion in his mouth. If you think that I—'

Twinks had hardly got started on her tirade when Baron Chipping Norton took a cravat out of his pocket and gagged her with it. Then he dragged her across to one of the metal pillars which supported the entire edifice of Tawcester Towers, forced her arms around it and clipped her wrists into handcuffs.

While the Baron was doing this, the plumber asked, 'Is the brother in custody too?'

'No,' came the rather peevish reply. 'This minx managed to spring him from Perylgrim Prison. I'm convinced Devereux Lyminster is still somewhere on the Tawcester Towers estate . . . though a police search this afternoon didn't find him. But the police – and the Tawcestershire Constabulary in particular – would be hard put to spot the kitten in a basket of puppies. Don't worry, I'll institute a far more efficient search shortly. Devereux Lyminster will not escape the majesty of British justice!'

The Baron looked at Twinks, who was visibly infuriated by her enforced dumbness. He smiled and said, 'The executions of you and your brother will serve as a warning to anyone else who tries to stem the advance of Aristotours. You are only concerned with your own property, Tawcester Towers. What you do not realise is the scale of the Aristotours enterprise. We are planning – and indeed close to – taking over all the stately homes of England and running 'How The Other Half Lives' events from them. We are meeting little opposition. Most of the peerage are so hopeless with money, so deeply in debt, that they welcome our approaches with open arms. That's certainly true of your mother, Lady Honoria. She couldn't have been happier to listen to our overtures. The Dowager Duchess has gone out of her way to assist our efforts.'

There were many articulate and crushing responses Twinks could have come up with in answer to all this, but the gag continued to curb her eloquence.

Enjoying his position of power, Baron Chipping Norton became even more triumphalist. 'And what, in spite of your much-vaunted intelligence, Lady Honoria, you would never have found out, was that Aristotours has a connection to an even more powerful association . . .'

'I know!' Twinks would have shouted, had shouting been an option. 'Razzy and I worked out the whole spoffing rombooley of your connection to the Secret Congregation of the Crooked Hand!'

'It is called,' revealed Baron Chipping Norton, 'the Secret Congregation of the Crooked Hand. And it is devoted to the cause of destroying all traditional institutions. Monarchies, governments, legal systems – none has a chance against the power of the Crooked Hand!'

Emboldened by his own rhetoric, the Baron raised the stakes. 'And I can tell you, Lady Honoria, because nobody will believe anything you say ever again, that things are about to change within the Secret Congregation of the Crooked Hand. You should know that the organisation's boss is given the title of "the Crooked Hand". But the current holder of that office has been – what shall I say – somewhat dilatory in moving along our agenda of destruction. I have taken soundings amongst the top management of Aristotours and, given that I have a private army of domestic staff at Paramere Castle, I now know that I am in a position to take over from the current incumbent of the office!

'So, Lady Honoria, how privileged you are! Your abduction this evening is the first action of . . . the new Crooked Hand!'

'Don't you think,' asked Rodney Perkins, in humble, artisan tones, 'that you ought to let the old Crooked Hand know before you take such a step?'

'Never!' cried Baron Chipping Norton. 'At the moment, my plans give me the advantage of surprise. Military commanders through the centuries have all recognised the advantage of surprise.'

'They certainly have!'

The voice which made this pronouncement was not that of a forelock-tugging plumber. Its tone was patrician and laced with pure evil. Rodney Perkins suddenly grew in stature as he moved at astonishing speed across the cellar floor. He snatched the revolver from the Baron's hand and, in a matter of seconds, had his wrists cuffed round a pillar, just as Twinks's had been.

'I think, Baron,' he said with icy precision, 'you would have been well advised to check with the incumbent before you tried to usurp the power of . . . the Crooked Hand!'

As he spoke the words, he pulled off a glove and raised his right hand to show that the fingers were misshapen, transformed into talons. Perhaps they had been like that all the time under the white gloves. At Tawcester Towers, nobody would have thought to look too closely at a plumber.

Baron Chipping Norton came out of shock to find his voice. 'You won't get away with this, Perkins!'

191

'Don't call me Perkins! I was never Perkins. My ancestry is far more distinguished. Certainly far more distinguished than yours, Chipping Norton.'

'Whatever you're called,' cried the Baron, 'your reign is over! My army of retainers will make short work of—'

So fast that it looked like one movement, the false plumber freed the cravat around Twinks's mouth and gagged the Baron with it. 'I already have got away with it!' announced the Crooked Hand, unchallenged in his supremacy.

'You're a Grade A foundation stone,' said a delighted Twinks, 'for getting me out of this gluepot. Now if you wouldn't mind decuffing my wristies . . .'

The look the Crooked Hand cast on her was not benign. 'I am sorry, Lady Honoria, if you believe me to be on a rescue mission. I'm afraid you're not going to find a Sir Galahad in this cellar. Instead, you are going to witness the greatest achievement to date of the Secret Congregation of the Crooked Hand!

'When I say that, I'm afraid you will only witness the beginning of that achievement. Sadly, you will not see the end.'

'You four-faced filcher!' cried Twinks. 'What back-door devilment are you planning? Was this why you pongled up to Tawcester Towers in the first place?'

'How well you understand, Lady Honoria. Tonight will witness the climax of an operation which has been years in the planning. I got the Secret Congregation of the Crooked Hand involved with Aristotours because our ambitions required the entrée to stately homes. And I played Aristotours along, pretending I would support their plans to turn ancestral piles into amusement arcades. The Crooked Hand also invested a lot in their schemes, but it was all to serve a greater purpose.

'This pathetic specimen . . .' He indicated Baron Chipping Norton '. . . mentioned the traditional targets of Anarchists – monarchies, governments and legal systems. But there was one bastion of privilege he missed out.' The Crooked Hand's expression grew even more evil, no longer retaining even the last vestige of plumberdom. 'He did not mention the aristocracy.'

'You lump of toadspawn!' shouted Twinks. 'I see the sneakery you've been practising. It was your suggestion to me that inviting the genuine article to this weekend would edge out the oikish sponge-worms, so that we'd end up with a Tawcester Towers full of Heirs Apparent!'

'Exactly. The cream of the heirs to most of the peerages in the country. If none of them gets out of this place alive, there'll be a good few empty seats in the House of Lords ... and a few more ancestral titles being inherited by distant cousins who've spent their lives sheep-farming in Australia.

'Yes, tonight will see the destruction of the British aristocracy! And the apotheosis of the Crooked Hand!'

'So, uncage the ferrets!' Twinks demanded boldly. 'How do you plan to work your wickedry? Since I'm not on the list of survivors, you don't need to have any squidges about telling me.'

'And indeed,' the smiling Crooked Hand responded, 'telling you will be an enormous pleasure, because you have shown some signs of knowing a bit about heating systems. So, I don't need to inform you that, in normal circumstances, an oil-fired boiler heats the water and pumps that hot water out into all the pipes and radiators to heat the rooms.'

'Tickey-tockey.'

'Well, I've made a slight refinement to that system. In fact, I was worried you might have caught on to it, when you came down here for a chat some time ago. Do you remember?'

'Like strawberries I do!'

'At that time, you suggested that I seemed to have rather an excessive amount of oil down here.'

'That bings the brain cells, yes.'

'Fortunately, you didn't pursue the thought, or I might have had to adjust my plans. Because, you see, for this evening only, rather than having water—'

'I'm ahead of you,' Twinks interposed. 'Rather than having water, you'll have oil being pumped round the system.'

'Well done, Lady Honoria! It is a pleasure to deal with such a quick mind. I am sorry that that pleasure will, inevitably, be so soon curtailed.'

'You bucket of bilge-water!' hissed Twinks.

'Anyway, I don't need to spell out any more of what will happen. I will set a fuse to the boiler . . . a long enough one for me to get safely off the premises. Then, when the boiler blows up, the oil in all the pipes and radiators will be ignited . . . the whole building will be a giant incendiary bomb . . .'

The Crooked Hand was brought together with the normal hand in a gesture of completion. 'Goodbye, Tawcester Towers! Goodbye, the entire next generation of the British aristocracy!'

Twinks was too overwhelmed to make any response.

'And there is nothing,' said the transmogrified plumber, as he bent down to light the long fuse, 'that anyone can do about it!'

'Don't you spoffing well believe that!' cried the voice of Blotto.

27

Derring-Done!

Maybe it had been some guardian angel – the spirit of Rupert the Cavalier, perhaps – which had woken Blotto up and led him through the endlessly interlocking cellars to the scene of his sister's jeopardy.

He arrived to be challenged by exactly the kind of odds he liked. Blotto, armed only with his cricket bat, faced the mastermind of an international Anarchist organisation, who already had the blood of many on his hands. The Crooked Hand was armed with Baron Chipping Norton's revolver, as well as a small arsenal of his own handguns. And he had just lit the fuse to an elaborate booby trap which would shortly blow Tawcester Towers and all inside the building to smithereens. Yes, Blotto relished the task ahead!

In the event, it was all over a lot quicker than he would have wished. And Blotto, uncharacteristically and to his huge regret, lost his temper.

He had come rushing towards his adversary, cricket bat at the ready. And the first bullet fired at him had embedded itself into treasured willow.

That was what had made Blotto lose his temper. He didn't care how many bullets got lodged in his own flesh, but for one to dig its way into his cricket bat ... When he thought of the many great innings the two of them had shared, when he thought of the hours he had spent lovingly rubbing linseed oil into the hallowed surface . . .

Blotto just thundered forward, knocking guns from the Crooked Hand and the unimpaired hand, and belabouring his opponent with the cricket bat the stencher had so sacrilegiously maltreated. In a matter of seconds, the man was sitting on the floor, dazed and incoherent.

Blotto was about to search the plumber's overalls for a handcuff key, but Twinks stopped him. 'It's in the other stencher's pocket,' she said.

Blotto raided Baron Chipping Norton's dinner jacket for what he wanted. He released his sister and, before the Crooked Hand was fully conscious, had him too handcuffed to one of the pillars.

'You really are the lark's larynx,' Twinks told her brother fondly.

'Shouldn't have lost the old bull-rag there,' he apologised. 'But when some slugbucket puts a bullet in a boddo's cricket bat . . .'

'Anyone would have done the same in your dancing pumps,' his sister reassured him.

'Good ticket, Twinks me old shrimp-filleter.'

'Fair biddles, Blotto me old knife-sharpener.'

'So, shall we rejoin the living?' he asked.

'One little thingette we ought to do first,' she said.

'And what's that when it's got its spats on?'

Twinks pointed to the cellar floor, where a spitting flame crept along the length of fuse which the Crooked Hand had so recently lit.

'Toad-in-the-hole!' said Blotto, as he went to stamp out the danger. For good measure, he pulled the other end out of the boiler.

Brother and sister smiled at each other. 'Shall we go upstairs and join the fireworks of fun?' suggested Twinks.

196

'Well, I don't know that I should,' said Blotto.

'Why, in the name of snitchrags, not?'

Blotto gestured to his tweed suit. 'Evening, isn't it? Haven't got the penguin togs on.'

Twinks was of the view that, after the international disaster he'd averted that evening, Blotto could, for once, cock a snook at convention.

As they were walking through the Tawcester Towers hallway, Blotto and Twinks were greeted by a very relieved-looking Grimshaw. 'Oh, milord, milady, how glad I am to have found you. The young gentlemen are getting rather impatient.'

'Which young gentlemen?' asked Twinks.

'All the young gentlemen who're here as guests for the weekend.'

'And why are they impatient?'

'They are waiting for your announcement, milady.'

'What announcement?'

The butler was not able to provide an answer to that question. Nor, it seemed, was a rather embarrassed-looking Blotto.

When they reached the Great Hall, Twinks was surprised to see it full of the Heirs Apparent, as if they had not moved since the end of the séance. In the chair where the supposed Signora Zucchini had sat, there was a very uncomfortable-looking Duke of Tawcester. Rupert the Insipid.

'Ah, there you are,' he said, with huge relief at his sister's appearance.

In a state of considerable bewilderment, Twinks allowed herself to be led down on to the stage. Applause and raucous cries welled up as she passed. Among the shouting could be heard several voices demanding, 'Tell us who it is, Twinks!'

When she reached her elder brother, she gave him a piercing look, hoping for some private explanation of what the hell was going on.

But when he did speak, he addressed not her, but the assembled Heirs Apparent.

'Gentlemen,' he cried. 'Erm . . . Now comes the moment you have all been waiting for. I know that you all came to Tawcester Towers this weekend for the same reason.' This was greeted by more raucous shouts. 'Fact is, you were all told that this evening, my sister, Lady Honoria Lyminster, would make an announcement as to which of you she was going to marry!'

Twinks focused a look of pure venom on her younger brother. He tried to make it clear, by facial expression alone, that he'd had to find some way to get all the Heirs Apparent to come to Tawcester Towers to prevent the weekend's places being taken up by oikish sponge-worms. But the human face is not up to communicating that much information.

So Blotto just turned away.

Having once again evaded commitment to marriage by her customary wiles, Twinks steamed through disappointed suitors in search of her younger brother, for whom she was preparing a dressing-down which would have prompted admiration – and even envy – from their mother.

But in the hallway, she found Blotto in the company of Sir Albert Anstruther. And, once again, handcuffed.

She went straight upstairs to her boudoir to fetch the dossier she had prepared on the crimes of Aristotours and, in particular, Baron Chipping Norton. She also took the dossier outlining the more extensive crimes of the Secret Congregation of the Crooked Hand, particularly featuring those committed by the Crooked Hand himself, a.k.a. Rodney Perkins.

When she rejoined the Chief Constable in the hallway, she not only handed him the dossiers, she also told him that the two main perpetrators were conveniently under restraint in the cellar.

Within an hour, all charges against Lord Devereux Lyminster had been dropped.

28

The Last Match of the Season

The Sunday suggested that September wasn't yet ready for autumn. Summer was too much fun to be abandoned so soon. As a result, it was a perfect day for the last cricket match of the season. Blotto hadn't had much difficulty in arranging the fixture that the Earl of Cleckheaton had suggested. A large number of the Heirs Apparent, so conveniently assembled at Tawcester Towers, had been his fellow muffin-toasters at Eton and were definitely up for a game. And the home team, led by Blotto, and with Corky Froggett as wicket-keeper, was always ready. So, many old memories were rekindled.

Blotto reminded everyone of his exceptional prowess, scoring an unbeaten double century, just as he had done in his Tawsworthy police station dream. His bowling figures had been pretty damned good too.

He looked forward, after the excitements of the last weeks, to a convivial dinner with some of his favourite old muffin-toasters. Though the Aristotours lot were all four-faced filchers and their main operators had been arrested, that evening's meal would still be under the departed Ulrich Weissfeder's influence, so he looked forward to excellent gorging and gulping.

Like the day, Blotto's personal barometer was firmly set to 'Sunny'.

Twinks also felt pleased with her achievements. She was confident that the dossiers she had compiled would destroy both Aristotours and the Secret Congregation of the Crooked Hand.

She was quite enthused by the prospect of getting back to her translation of *Three Men in a Boat* into the Mongolic Khalkha dialect. She still hadn't found a Khalkha expression that carried all the nuances of 'Irish stew'. But she'd get there.

It was also a relief that she hadn't ended the weekend engaged to one of the Heirs Apparent. Announcing that she was going to become a nun had perhaps been an extreme measure, but at least it got her off the hook in the short term. Being a 'bride of God' would keep her safe for the time being, and she felt that, when the moment was right, God would be understanding about her breaking off the engagement.

She did have a one-to-one with her mother in the Blue Morning Room about the whole Aristotours experience. The Dowager Duchess claimed that she'd recognised them as shysters from the start. She had only gone along with their plans because she saw a cunning way of getting Tawcester Towers' heating problem sorted – and having the great house refurbished – at Aristotours's expense.

Twinks recognised that all of this was completely untrue. The Dowager Duchess would have sold the entire family down the river without a flicker of conscience.

But, whatever her original motives, Twinks could not deny that much of the outcome had been good. The central heating system, once all the oil had been flushed out and replaced by hot water, would keep Tawcester Towers warm through many a winter.

The improvements to the bedrooms were a definite bonus, too. And Twinks felt sure that, in time, in the ancestral moistness of the old building, the new sheets would get damp, just like sheets in an English stately home should be.

Around Tawcester Towers, things settled down.

The collapse of Aristotours had seen the swift departure of Ulrich Weissfeder and his acolytes. Life below stairs returned to its former serenity. The ruffled green baize on the dividing door was once again smoothed down. Grimshaw, restored to his domestic eminence, still refused to make an honest woman of Harvey. But his satisfaction at the return of the *status quo* did allow the smallest flicker to manifest itself on his right eyebrow. Once.

Until such time as the demand came for him to lay down his life for the young master, Corky Froggett continued to polish the Lagonda to within an inch of its life. And he continued to escort kitchen maids along the tunnel from the great house to his specially equipped hayloft.

After the excitements of a murder investigation, Chief Inspector Trumbull and Sergeant Knatchbull returned to their customary state of perpetual bafflement. And they had the unexplained hole in the roof of their police station repaired.

The investigations into Baron Chipping Norton and the Crooked Hand ended, appropriately and conveniently (for loose-end-tying-up) on the gallows.

And, in due time, Sloggo gave birth to another girl.